BEAUTIFUL BOYS

BEAUTIFUL BOYS

GAY EROTIC STORIES

EDITED BY
RICHARD LABONTÉ

CLEIS
PRESS

Published in the United States by Cleis Press Inc., 2246 Sixth Street, Berkeley, California 94710.

Printed in the United States.
Cover design: Scott Idleman
Cover photograph: Martin San/Getty Images
Text design: Frank Wiedemann
Cleis logo art: Juana Alicia
First Edition.
10 9 8 7 6 5 4 3 2 1

ISBN: 978-1-57344-412-5

Asa,
through two decades
my Beautiful ~~Boy~~ Man

Contents

INTRODUCTION: EYE OF THE BEHOLDER

Though one man's beauty might well be another man's beast, the reality is that queer fellows—at least stereotypically—most often place a premium on model good looks and well-toned bodies. And so it is with a few of the stories in *Beautiful Boys*: the idealized man, or better yet one man's idealized man, depicted for your sensual delectation.

But I also sought stories with more than head-turning outer beauty, radiant good looks, scorching physical appeal, or the twinky youth of a porn performer. I wanted writing that depicted men whose eye-of-the-beholder magnificence was balanced by the character of the man within: cuties who were more than merely objects of desire.

And I wanted contributors to stretch the standard queer definition of beauty. For Rob Wolfsham, for example, the attraction is to scruffy lads; with Barry Lowe, the narrative is about attraction to men damaged by their perfection; in a mini-memoir, Andy Quan remembers a gym acquaintance, long lusted after, who died for his beauty; and in another mini-memoir, Dan Cullinane recalls the men he has desired, or who have desired him, men of varied beauty and even men he lived with "who I never wanted to touch."

Beautiful boys: no one perfect size fits all.

In my domestic relationship life, beauty is almost an afterthought. I'm as likely as the next gay man to have his head turned by a stunner, and like most gay men I have my ideals—lithe body, prominent nose, reddish hair, toned muscle.

Truth is, happily, none of my long-term partners have been all that. Norman's hair was reddish, but mostly after an application of henna. Fernando was willowy, but his nose was a treat. Rhonda, my fairy-named love, has grown into the kind of man he fancied when we met—chubby is the affectionate term of choice. And Asa, a laborer all his life, arrived in my home toned and tall, but shorn of hair. Together they, and assorted boyfriends along the way, add up to a composite of my ideal guy. But their shared appeal for me was (and is) a singular inner beauty, the best aphrodisiac of all, the basis for our being united (serially) in love over four decades.

Beautiful men: they come in all shapes and sizes. That's real life.

Richard Labonté
Bowen Island, British Columbia

THE RAFT RACE

Phillip Mackenzie, Jr.

Jim walked over to the fire and tossed a load of branches onto it, and sparks rocketed through the cold night toward the wash of the Milky Way above. I was talking to Noah, my back to the fire, and I jumped about a half foot in the air and yelled, "Fuck me," right into his face. He laughed, and we turned around to face the fire, and through the flames and smoke, one of his little girls in his arms and a leather hat pulled down over his brow, I saw the only guy I ever loved.

Twenty years on and nothing in common but a childhood tossed into the years, I wondered if I should even bother saying hello. But Richie saw me, too, and he chucked his chin in my direction and set the little girl down. April, I think someone had told me her name was. I had heard that he and his wife had moved down to Portland for a couple of years, had a few more kids and then moved back up to Idaho where opportunities were scarce but the faces were familiar.

We grew up here, on adjacent pieces of land. Our mothers hewed to this place with the fervor born of the back-to-nature movement of the sixties and seventies. Richie had a twin brother, Joey, and the three of us clung together as we survived all manner of well-meaning progressive experiments, like home-schooling, self-sufficiency farming, organic gardening and goats' milk. When we hit adolescence we begged to be normal.

Joey was as still and watchful as Richie was restless and watch-spring wound up. Goofus and Gallant brought to life, when Richie and I would stroll out the door of the Safeway, our pockets and pants fronts stuffed with Cadbury bars and *Mad* magazines, we would find Joey waiting, twisting with remorse at our bad behavior.

We came off our farms at fourteen and uncertainly joined the world. High school was like a foreign country to us. By our sophomore year, Richie was downing two or three beers behind the wheel of his pickup, as the three of us rode the gravel road to school buzzed and hypersensitive. He picked fights almost every day. Joey and I made excuses to the people he punched out or puked on, and we laughed with him to make him feel like he was okay, but it didn't get any better, and after awhile I started making up excuses about other things I had to do, and after awhile I did have other things to do.

Joey stuck by Richie and looked at me with big hurt eyes as I drifted away from them. We sat on the sagging old gate in their barnyard one night, our breath coming out clouds in the cold, and I told him that Richie scared me. "He scares everyone, Joey. People think he's nuts. They think he's dangerous, and they think he's a drunk."

Joey just smiled. "He's okay."

When we passed each other in the hallway at school, Richie and I would nod or say hi, but not much more. Every time it happened was like a kick in the stomach, but when you're the one who started the kicking, how do you stop it?

* * *

I stopped growing in my junior year, but Richie and Joey got bigger and bigger. They worked summers when they could for one or the other of the logging outfits in town. They struggled through brush on steep hillsides setting cables on felled trees, which would be yanked upward by winches. The work was brutal and dangerous, and I pictured them doing it: Richie crashing through undergrowth like a bull, with Joey behind him trying to keep him safe.

By our senior year, they were both over six-four; standing side by side in the hallway, their shoulders almost touched the lockers lining the walls. They should have played football, but the coach was afraid Richie would kill someone, and Joey wasn't going to go where his brother wasn't wanted. That whole year, I barely spoke to them. Richie was lost to something I couldn't understand, and so it was easier to let him go. But Joey broke my heart.

I saw them at graduation. Our moms forced us together for a photograph, me in the middle, the brothers towering over me, their massive arms over my shoulders. I never saw the picture. A few weeks later, Joey called.

"We're gonna do the raft race this summer," he said, the question hanging but not asked.

I wanted to say yes. I knew I would say yes. But I wasn't sure if he'd ask, and it seemed like way too much to assume.

"We could use some help. You know, a third guy to help steer," he paused, "Or build. You know."

I suppose he was hoping that if the three of us did something together, like back when we were eleven and tried to build a cabin up in the woods above the dairy farm, it would make the last four years disappear. I suppose I was hoping for the same thing, because I said yes.

The raft race was pretty badly named, because the rafts barely floated, and they sure didn't race. But it was the kickoff event for Kootenai River Days, the town's annual summer festival. About fifty teams of local guys whacked together a flotilla of crappy rafts and drifted ten miles or so down the Kootenai in a long drunken party, until whoever still had a raft holding together long enough to accidentally drift into town first was declared the winner. Sometimes there was a guy who took it seriously and paddled like a Harvard oarsman, but everyone just laughed at him until he relaxed. It's not like there was a prize. I think the winner got a hundred dollar gift certificate to Coast to Coast or Tafts.

I should have thought about it. I should have known that Richie wasn't doing it for fun. I should have known he had something to prove.

Richie and Joey were setting chokers for Pruitt's and I was working up at Clifty View Nursery, so we met in the putrid dinginess of Mr. C's on Main Street, where under-thirty drunks in training hung out to shoot pool and listen to bad covers of Eagles songs. We knocked back a few beers and then wandered down the street to the Panhandle Café for burgers.

It would be great to say it was just like old times, but that would be bullshit. Richie and I could barely look at each other. We never talked about how we had been like brothers, and now we weren't even friends. So that fact sat in the middle of the table like a stain while we avoided each other's eyes and talked through Joey. But from that night, a raft was born.

It turned out to be a fairly complex design of PVC piping, inner tubes and pallet wood. The PVC piping was sealed up at either end and served as the framework to hold it all together. The inner tubes were effectively caged inside this and covered with more PVC; the pallet wood was for the platform and for the railings we envisioned leaning on as we swept victoriously into town.

From the planning stage through the construction of our raft, the three of us reconnected in a way that was still misshapen. I laughed at Richie's jokes and put up with him picking me up and bench-pressing me over his head.

"You're such a skinny little punk," he said, his voice not even a little bit warm.

"Fuck you, Frankenstein." I said, and Joey winced, but Richie laughed and tossed me a beer.

We sat side by side on the tailgate of Richie's pickup looking at our raft. The sun stretched toward the mountains, across fields tall with alfalfa. The smell of summer was heavy, and suddenly I wanted to cry. My throat felt like a chunk of granite was lodged there, and as I fought it down, I looked sideways at Joey who was kicking at the dust with one booted toe. This was what it could be, but it could never be what it should have been.

We launched our raft into the brown swirling water of the river just a little after ten A.M and exited the race about twenty-five minutes later. The bungee cords we used to hold the PVC framework together started sagging fast, and the whole thing began to fall apart after about a mile. At about a mile and a half, the inner tubes broke free and floated off on their own, and we were left in the middle of the river, clinging to our craft like rats on a pile of pick-up sticks. The laughter from the last of the rafts struggling past us had barely faded as we struggled ashore, dragging our crumbling cage, and collapsed on the muddy bank.

Richie sat in the mud for barely a second, before getting to his feet and screaming, "Fuck!" at the top of his lungs. As Joey and I watched, he kicked the remains of the raft into pieces, occasionally stopping to pick up a shard or two of PVC and hurl it into the scrub grass along the banks of the river. His rage was silent after his first explosion. Joey dropped his head between his knees, and his shoulders sagged.

I wanted to scream at Richie. "It's just a stupid fucking raft, you idiot. It doesn't mean anything."

Joey got up and said in a flat voice, "Richie, give me the keys."

Richie whirled on him, a piece of pallet wood in his hand. "What?"

"The keys. To the truck. I'm gonna drive it down here."

"Why?"

Because he wants to get away from you, I thought, but Joey only said "Because."

They stared at each other for a moment, and then Richie fished into his soaked jeans and pulled out his keys. "Watch second. It sticks."

After Joey left, Richie sat on a log a few yards away. I leaned back on the clay bank, and listened to the water swirling toward town without us.

"Fuck. Fuck. Fuck. Fuck." Richie said softly.

I leaned on my elbows and looked over at him. His eyes were closed, and he had pulled his soaked T-shirt off. Snake grass rose up around his legs and sweating torso. He was logger pale, brown arms and face ending with a slash into marble white. He became still and he was quiet, but tension coiled off him in the stark tendons and hardened ropes of muscle that wrapped his body.

He opened his eyes and found me watching him.

"What?"

"Nothing."

He got off the log and walked toward me. "Don't say *nothing*. What?"

"Why do you have to...?" I trailed off. "Never mind."

He was standing over me and reached down and grabbed me by the front of my shirt and pulled me off the ground.

"Why do I have to what?"

I scrabbled with my toes for ground and grabbed at his arm. "What are you gonna do, Richie, kick me to pieces, too?"

"Fuck you." He dropped me and turned away, then whirled back toward me and advanced to within a few inches. "I should kick the shit out of you. I should. I should fucking kill you."

I stepped back, shaking my head. "Go ahead, I don't give a shit what you do. Go ahead."

He stared at me, and then his eyes were full of tears. I watched, horrified, as he stood in front of me and started to cry.

"Yeah," he spat out, his voice choked. "Yeah, I know that."

He towered over me, the top of my head barely reaching the hollow of his throat. This mountain of a man with whom I had once run through the world stood in front of me, his chest hiccupping and trembling. I was frozen. Then he whirled away and walked to the river. He kicked off his muddy shoes and shucked out of his soaking jeans and, naked, hurled himself into the brown eddying water.

When he surfaced he stood, water streaming in rivers down the landscape of his nakedness, splitting apart over bulging muscles and coming back together over the flatness of his hard stomach, and he walked out of the water, and I felt something tear apart inside me and I started shaking.

"I had a friend once," he said, his voice high and clear, "and then I didn't. All those years, back when we were freaks, we were always side by side. I guess I thought that meant something."

"What do you mean? We weren't freaks."

"Yeah we were. Little hippy kids that didn't go to school, running around in hand-me-down clothes, while our moms walked around town in patched jeans and long skirts. What do you think people thought?"

"I don't know. I don't care. We were just kids. Besides, that changed."

"Yeah. Yeah, it really changed. You got too good for us."

"That's not what happened."

He snorted and ran his hand across his head, brushing his dripping hair out of his eyes.

"You didn't want to know me. That's what happened."

After all this time, we're finally having the conversation, and he's standing there naked, water shining on his skin, so close to me I can feel the heat coming off him. My mouth was dry as I tried to form sticky words.

"You changed. I didn't change. You changed. You…"

"What? I what?"

"You went fucking crazy, Richie. Insane. Drunk and starting shit all the time. I don't know what happened to you and neither did Joey." I was shouting before I realized it. "You were scary to be around."

"You sound like a fucking girl."

"Why did you do that shit?" I ignored him, "Why were you pissed off all the time?"

"Because I didn't want to fucking be there," he roared at me. "I didn't want to give up everything that was cool about us and figure out how to be them."

Goddamn it. And I knew that, too. I wasn't so stupid I couldn't figure that out. I was on the edge of knowing what I did when I pulled back.

"You should put some clothes on."

He looked down at himself and then burst out laughing.

"Oh, the hell with it," he said and turned his back to me and walked toward where his clothes were piled on the bank.

"I'm sorry," I said under my breath, but he heard me all the same.

"Yeah, so what," he muttered, his back still toward me. "You got what you wanted."

"I didn't know what to do." I said more loudly. "I didn't know how to be when I was around you."

He swung around, his jeans dangling from his hands and then stalked toward me.

"Be around me? What the hell does that mean? We'd been around each other all our lives." Then he hit me with his pants. It was so stupid, him swinging his wet jeans into my face, but they hit me like a log. For a second I was stunned, his voice shouting in my ear.

"You didn't want to be around me because I didn't fit in. You got as far away from me as fast as you could before I even had a chance to figure out what was going on."

That wasn't true, I knew it, and he knew it. But it was true. Inside me where he couldn't get, I knew it was true.

I had staggered back when he hit me, and now I came at him from a crouch, caught him around the middle and took both of us flying into the river. It was the only answer I had for what he had said.

Richie went down on his back in the river with a loud smack, me on top of him, clutching at his naked writhing form. He locked his arms around my waist and pulled me tight into him. I was soaked through, and I could feel every inch of him pressing into me. He rolled me over, pushing my head under the water. Through the cloudy swirling river, he flickered and wavered above me, like a phantom.

Then he was pulling me out and tossing me like a sack toward the shore. I landed, sprawling into the mud, scrambling with my hands up the slope, my feet slipping out behind me. He yanked me up again and whirled me around to face him, his fist already swinging toward my head. When it connected it felt like he ripped half my nose off, and the blood start flowing.

I fell backward, the neck of my shirt ripping in his hands, and as I fell I kicked out as hard as I could, catching him somewhere by his ankle and sending him off balance. As I landed on my back, I saw him stumble and land on one knee. I rolled as fast as I could in the other direction, but he was up and on me before I got anywhere.

"Stop it," he was saying, his knee in my back. "Stop it, don't. Don't."

"You fucking hit me," I screamed, my face inches from the mud. "*You* stop it."

I lay in the mud and he took his knee off my back and knelt beside me. He put his hand on my shoulder and we sat there, breathing hard, and then he was pulling me up, cradling me in his massive arms, my head pressed against his muddy chest.

"I never wanted to do that," he whispered. "Ever."

I looked up at him. His face was worried.

When we were twelve, I fell off a runaway horse and broke my arm. I had screamed and rolled over cradling my arm and seen legs racing toward me across the field. Richie had landed on his knees next to me, rolled me over and lifted me into his lap, staring down at me. Now his face was a terrifying shadow of that, and all that had been thrown away crashed down and flattened me, and I started sobbing.

"Goddamn it, Richie," I choked out. "Goddamn it."

He wiped tears off my face and pulled me into a hug. I put my arms around him and started crying harder. He put his hand on the back of my head, pressing my face into his neck.

* * *

Looking back on this, all these years later, I know we didn't mean it to happen. It wasn't something that had always been there. Truly. We were just raw. We were only kids, really, even though Richie was wrapped inside the massive body of something more. When he kissed my cheek, it was meant as comfort, but I turned my head in surprise and his mouth was still just there. His lips came down again, and I met him straight on, and all the air in the world went away, and my heart was in a pinching vise as I breathed him into me.

So, we didn't stop. We kept going. There was too much space between us, every fraction of an inch of air became more than we could bear. Every bit of clothing I was wearing was too much. His skin was slippery and then mine was, too. The sun played over us, and the river danced, and our lips never left each other's.

I was naked and on my knees in front of him, his hands on either side of my face. Rigid and throbbing flesh spanned the distance, and when I felt the spongy head of his dick brush my lips, I didn't hesitate. Too much space, this air between us. I opened my mouth and he slid inside me, over my tongue and on back.

He murmured something inarticulate and gently pulled my face forward until my bleeding nose was buried in the river-smelling forest of hair between his legs.

I could have sucked his cock forever. My heart hammered in shock as I slobbered over the head, running my tongue over the ridge of the crown, burying it in the gaping, weeping slit, then down the veiny shaft until my forehead was pressed again against the ridged rockiness of his stomach.

But Richie pulled me up, pulled me closer, ridding us of unwanted inches. I stared into his eyes as we went to the ground together. He stared back as I moved on top of him, straddling him, reaching behind me and finding him. We struggled together to find a way to get rid of this last unwanted space between us. There was spit, and there was pressure and a searing pain that made me feel like everything could be good again. Then he was sliding into me and saying my name and grabbing my head and pulling me in for a kiss.

We sat like that for a moment, scared and breathing in catches. Then Richie shifted, and a look almost like pain crossed his face.

"I'm sorry," he said, "but I have to do this."

He pushed into me the rest of the way, and I arched my back so hard I thought I might break.

Then it was fury. He rolled me onto my back, pulling almost all the way out of me. He hovered over me, his face as open as a child's, his broad chest corded with muscles stretched as taut as cables. Then he slammed forward and lifted his head and opened his mouth in a scream that emerged as only a sigh. Every inch was gone. We were fused.

I remember pain breaking into something else, and then he couldn't be far enough inside me. I wrapped everything I had around him and pulled him deeper. Every unspoken word that had passed between us as our eyes met in the high school hallway poured into that moment on the riverbank, with the mud squelching around our bodies and the sun beating down and slicking us with sweat. We were making sounds, but I don't know if they were words. Those inches, inches, inches, all of his inches, all of them inside me. Him. His body. His sweat mingling with mine. His arms around me. His mouth on mine again and again. And the never stopping, never slowing, rhythm of the connection we had made.

Then chaos and shattering savage thrusts, and then Richie was rolling backward, me fully shanked on him, his huge calloused hands finding me and pulling ribbon after ribbon of heat out of me. I couldn't breathe or move, I could only watch as I sprayed all over him, white droplets running down his chest in streams to the place where we were still connected, giving him a slippery path to move even faster inside me. His thighs slammed into the back of my legs, and I clamped my palms down on them, feeling the muscles straining against my hands.

And he was still. His hand grabbed at the back of my head and pulled my face toward his. His mouth latched on to mine, and he groaned deep into me. Inside me, I felt him swell and break apart as the first blast of heat shot toward my heart. There were more, but that first one, the first shot, hit me hardest, this thing he was leaving inside me. It was him. And now it was mine.

After that, there wasn't anything to say. We couldn't talk about it. We clung to it for as long as we could, but I could feel him slipping out of me. Silently, we walked into the river and washed. We stood on the riverbank naked and looked at each other, knowing that the thing that made this possible would never happen again. If it did, it would be something else, and rather than draw us closer, it would drive us apart. So we dressed.

Richie returned to his log, and we silently surveyed the wreckage of our raft.

"You know, that…" he pointed at what was left. "That was Joey's idea."

"I know."

"You gonna tell him?"

"Are you?"

"I don't see why."

Joey came clomping up the riverbank a few minutes later, and the three of us walked back to where he had parked the truck. Joey didn't say anything when he saw the blood around my nose, but he shot a look over at Richie and then back at me to see if we'd tell him. We didn't. To tell him that would be to tell him everything. When I saw him, I felt like I had betrayed him, but there was no way to share this.

We stopped in town for a beer.

"Our raft was the worst one, I think," Joey said.

"Probably," Richie said. "You think there's a prize for that?"

I lifted my beer, "To truly shitty rafts."

Richie nodded, and raised his beer. "I'll drink to that."

"You'll drink to anything," Joey said and then raised his beer. "Shitty rafts forever."

But there was no forever. The summer drifted by, and all I saw of Richie was the shape of him behind the wheel of his truck, a hand lifted in greeting as we passed each other on the county road. As for the inevitable moving on and moving away, I never said good-bye, and whatever space I left behind became something I never thought about.

When I returned, for Christmas or sometimes in summer, the space I filled was something new. I heard about marriages and children, but I never tried to connect, and the pile of years became too large to climb over.

But Richie was walking around the fire, his eyes on me, and I didn't look away. Somewhere inside me, there was something of him. We still owned each other.

BOY CURATION

Rob Wolfsham

U ri Vitko pointed a large, black DSLR camera with a lens like a cannon at Rich Smith, his presently shirtless boyfriend of one week. Rich was a lithe, scruffy twenty-one-year-old with buzzed blond hair and a pierced eyebrow and lip. A cigarette scrunched and glowing down to the filter drooped from his bottom lip. The bones of his spine bisected a vulture tattoo, brown wings spread across his shoulder blades. He stirred a pot of chicken stew on the stove. Steam joined cigarette smoke and the aroma of curry. His left arm had a sleeve tattoo of a steel blue eagle, feathers fluttering down his skin and veins, merging into silver scales of a viper coiled around a dull yellow skull resting on his wrist. His earlobes accommodated two-gauge black rings.

The shutter clicked two times.

Rich glanced at the large lens several feet away. The shutter clicked two more times.

"You should cook shirtless more often," Uri said, voice muffled as he looked down at the LCD screen, reviewing the last image of Rich's pale tattooed body, straw goatee and blue eyes in gold light. "This is going to get so many likes, a hot indie boy who can cook."

"Don't upload that," Rich said smashing his cigarette in the sink. "I look like shit. And don't call me indie. Don't call anything indie."

"I'm not going to put all of them up," Uri said. "Maybe like three. Don't be so label phobic."

"Don't be so identitarian," Rich said, one eyebrow vaulting at Uri.

"The Internet needs labels. Tags. It's how people find my blog, the one you never look at." The shutter clicked again.

"Internet's evil," Rich said. He leaned over the pot and sipped from his spoon, frowning thoughtfully, chin and goatee pushed out. The shutter clicked and caught his expression in the lens.

Uri looked up from the little glowing screen. "That's like saying cars are evil. The Internet is just a vehicle for content."

"Cars *are* evil. Jesus."

Uri started walking away. "I'm uploading these now."

"Wait, babe." Rich held a big spoonful of soup toward Uri. "Try this."

Uri leaned over, black shoulder-length hair falling over his square Eastern European face. He slurped from the spoon. "Too salty. Wait, hold on." Uri set the camera in macro mode and held the lens up to the quivering spoon, almost touching. The spoon came into razor sharp focus, each pearl of broth and saliva glistening. Rich stood blurry in the background at a dramatic angle. The shutter clicked.

Rich dunked the spoon in the pot. "Now you're being ridiculous." He tried to grab the camera from Uri, but Uri wouldn't let go. Rich pulled him close against his pale inked body. Uri tugged on the camera again, then pressed his nose into the nook of

Rich's neck and shoulder where blue feathers tapered off. They both cradled the camera. Rich smelled like smoke and curry. He grinned at Uri like a joker with curling dimples. His teeth were slightly crooked with canines a little too sharp. Uri's nose slid up Rich's neck to his blond chin scruff, then his lips. They kissed and tongued each other. The lens of the camera prodded Rich's ribs as Uri pressed his crotch against the subject of his photography, the bones of their knees under their jeans rolling over each other.

"Don't be shy," Uri said against Rich's jugular vein.

"I'm not," Rich purred and let go of the camera to unbuckle Uri's jeans. He yanked the belt out like a whip and turned the stove to low. With the devotion of a famished wolf, he tore apart the fly of Uri's jeans and yanked them down hairless thighs. He folded to his knees and buried his nose in the bulge of Uri's blue briefs, sniffing and mouthing the soft cock under the fabric. His lip piercing rolled over the cotton where the head of Uri's cock pulsed.

Uri gritted his teeth and smeared his palm on the kitchen counter. Rich snuck his hand through the gap between Uri's thighs and palmed the back of his balls. He rubbed his middle finger into the soft stretch cotton against Uri's asshole.

Uri moaned and leaned against the counter and held the camera up to his face, pointing the lens down at Rich's eager lips.

Rich rubbed the fabric of Uri's underwear into his hole, gnawing on the cock straining against cotton. He heard the click of a shutter and looked up, grinning but with eyebrows furrowed.

"Don't be shy," Uri said.

"I'm not when I'm off the record," Rich said, latching his thumbs under the brim of Uri's briefs. He pulled them down and let Uri's firm five inches breathe inside his mouth. Rich's tongue shined and slurped Uri's uncut cock, lips slipping fast from head down to hairless base. The warm ring in Rich's bottom lip rolled over vein and foreskin. Rich pulled off. The strong male tang and scent of Uri's uncut cock overpowered the curry and spices of the kitchen.

"You're fresh," Rich said, a string of saliva connecting his lip ring to Uri's foreskin.

"Sorry, I need to shower," Uri said. He still held the camera in his sweaty hands, the shaft of the lens aimed at the detail of the saliva bridge between his foreskin and Rich's mouth.

"No, I like it. Shower less often." Rich sucked his own middle finger to the base and snuck his hand between Uri's thighs again. His wrist pressed against the taint behind Uri's balls, and he rubbed his middle finger against the hairless hole, sneaking in.

Uri sucked in air and parted his legs, squatting into the hand. Rich gulped down the slick cock while curling his bony middle finger into Uri's warmth, sliding in second-knuckle deep, clutching him closer in his palm.

Uri groaned as Rich took his cock down his throat and slid the tip of his finger around Uri's pulsing prostate. Rich mashed his sharp nose into Uri's smooth navel. He swallowed his length down, swishing his head around to attack the uncut cock from all angles with his tongue. Uri dragged his nails through Rich's prickly buzzed hair. Rich gagged and the back of his tongue gulped against the underside of Uri's cock with each slurp and gurgle. Uri growled and Rich recognized the need and shoved his middle finger deeper into his boyfriend, flicking around his insides, at the same time grabbing the base of his cock and jacking him furiously, tonguing his slit and foreskin.

"Fuck, I'm gonna cum," Uri moaned and held his breath in his throat, lips parted, still aiming the camera lens at the tongue worming under his foreskin. His ass clenched the finger inside him. Spurts of a four-day load seared through his cock with each pump of Rich's fist. Spunk filled Rich's mouth, spilling out the corners and smearing across his lips. Rich swallowed what he could. A spurt of cum webbed into his lip ring. He rubbed his middle finger around Uri's quivering prostate, wheedling what leftovers he could before he slid out and polished his finger with a dish towel. Uri shuddered in post-orgasmic delight; he couldn't resist when Rich grabbed the camera from his hand and deleted pictures on the memory card one by one.

"Come on," Uri exhaled, shoulders slumping.

Rich turned the camera on Uri. "If you need to remember anything, just ask." The camera flashed, blinding Uri for an instant.

Uri mashed his hair against his face. "No, no pictures of me."

"Don't like it?" Rich grinned mischievously and poked the lens right up to Uri's eyes. The camera flashed again.

Uri snatched the camera from him. "Cut it out. You're going to fuck up the lens."

Rich shrugged and picked up a potato on the counter and started peeling it over the sink, stifling his smile.

Uri set the camera on the counter and moved behind Rich. He leaned against Rich's back, pressing his cheek against the face of the vulture on his spine. He pulled his jeans and boxers down, finding no resistance from Rich. Uri got on his knees and ate out Rich's fuzzy blond ass and balls, reaching around to stroke seven cut inches. Uri returned the orgasmic favor as Rich cooked their dinner with a pleased smile.

The next night Uri took Rich barhopping with friends. It was the heart of December, the air raw, sidewalks slushy with old snow. Uri's friend Marcus had just graduated the day before. It was a Friday night. Their group of twelve guys ran through the bar district of their college town in a wet fog, bar to bar down the red-brick street. They crossed paths with other groups of reveling December graduates. Uri's friends were a sharper bunch than Rich, wealthy boys from the big city, wearing sherbet, collared shirts and stonewashed jeans. Rich stuck out with his piercings and black Killswitch Engage hoodie. He straggled several feet behind the crowd with a cigarette perched on his lips. Uri stayed back with him.

"What do you think of my friends?" Uri asked on the edge of laughter, black eyes wide with curious expectation.

"They're nice," Rich said taking a drag from his cigarette, other hand tucked in his hoodie pocket.

"You're not really talking to them," Uri said.

They marched down the sidewalk. Rich kept his eyes on the terrain of slushy ice under his boots. "They're not really talking to me."

"Just loosen up, have fun."

"Bars like Klusoz and Melt aren't really my places."

"Would you rather we go to Adolf's and get our asses kicked?"

"I'd protect you." Rich blew smoke over his shoulder and clutched Uri's neck, lightly shaking him. The question was flawed since Rich would never set foot in a dive like Adolf's. Uri still had an assumptive naivety about him. He wasn't as *hard* as he'd like to think.

Up ahead the guys tried to quiet Marcus, a chubby guy wearing a bright red Lacoste shirt. He was shouting the chorus of "Bad Romance" by Lady Gaga at the top of his lungs, stumbling across the street toward a bar called the Library, which looked to be the loudest, most crowded joint on the street.

Rich flicked his cigarette into a puddle of ice. "But those guys would be on their own."

Jason, a taller, muscular jock wearing a bright teal polo swung around and snapped a photo of Rich and Uri with his iPhone while walking backward. "Rich, I'm going to add you on Facebook," he said with missionlike determination. Jason's hair was bleach blond and spiky, his skin tanned into bronze. He was gorgeous with classic boy-next-door cheekbones and a button nose.

"I don't have a Facebook," Rich said.

"Oh, my god, are you fucking kidding?"

"No, I'm not on the Internet."

"But you're all over Uri's blog."

Rich gave Uri a nonplussed smile, nodding with a knowingness of *I am aren't I?*

"So you're not a student," Jason said unable to hide the slight disparaging tone in his voice. "What do you do?"

Rich coughed some smoke. "Practice being broke." He grinned at Jason, but his eyes weren't in it.

"Hey, it's all good, Uri doesn't have a job either."

"Thanks, Jason," Uri said.

"Why don't you put some ads on your blog?" Jason asked. "With all your viewers, you could make cum loads of money. Rich, you should get a decent cut since you're on there so much."

"I feel like I'd lose some of the artistry if I did that," Uri said. "I don't want to tarnish Rich's anarchist image."

"My anarchist image?" Rich asked, surprised.

"Yeah, speaking of which, one of those images last night, over a hundred people commented or liked it."

"What image?" Rich asked.

"The one where you're in your boxers adjusting the digital antenna."

"I told you not to upload that one. You can see my asscrack."

Uri shrugged high, averting his eyes. "You have no idea how striking you are."

"You *are* hot!" Jason chirped, still walking backward pointing his iPhone at Rich. "You should be happy to join the boys that Uri curates. You're like this punk, fuck-everything guy. I wouldn't even guess you were gay. I love your piercings. Did the lip one hurt?"

"Yeah, it did."

Jason poked around his phone with his thumb. "Uri, I just uploaded that first pic to Facebook and tagged you."

"Rich, show Jason your tattoos," Uri said. "Rich has these awesome tattoos."

Rich rolled up the left sleeve of his hoodie, showing off his steel blue feathers, silver python and yellow skull.

"Awesome, I have a tattoo, too!" Jason spun around and lifted the back of his shirt. Black scripted letters right above his asscrack spelled IXOYE. "I just got it. It's Greek for Jesus."

"You're religious?" Rich asked.

"Hell, yeah. Jesus is my inspiration for everything." Jason aimed his iPhone at Rich's arm. "You should do porn. You have such a look. Uri could help you, little photo bug that he is. He took all my modeling shots."

"Um, no," Rich said. "That doesn't interest me at all."

"Jason is actually a porn star," Uri said.

"I've only done like three movies," Jason said, nonchalantly flexing his biceps over his head. He stepped backward off the curb into the street.

"He's being modest," Uri said. "One of the movies he's in won a GayVN."

"I don't know what that means," Rich said.

"It's like the Oscars for porn."

"It helps pay for nursing school," Jason said. "And it's so

nice to get flown out of Lubbock on weekends to film. But after two more semesters, I'm done with it."

"Tired of feeling like an object?" Rich asked.

"Why would I feel like an object?" Uri grabbed Rich's arm, "Show Jason the vulture tattoo on your back."

"It's like twenty degrees out here," Rich said.

"C'mon," Uri pleaded.

"Maybe when we're inside."

Jason spun around and joined up with the crowd of guys across the street.

After they crossed the icy street, Uri stopped Rich. Green neon lights on the side of the building cast a sickly glow on Rich's sharp, tired face. "What's wrong?" Uri asked.

"Nothing." Rich scratched his neck. "Let's just go."

"Home?"

"Yeah."

"It's only midnight," Uri said.

Rich pulled his hood over his head and cupped Uri's jaw, pulling him into a kiss. He said against his lips, "Let's just get away from them and fuck."

Uri kissed back. "Okay."

"Hey!" came a husky voice. Marcus, the stocky new graduate of the group, playfully shoved Uri, knocking him off Rich. "None of that out here, faggots, unless you want a hate crime."

The guys were scattering and Marcus told the two that the Library was too crowded so they were all headed back to his house. "Y'all coming?"

"Yeah!" Uri chimed, tugging Rich's sweater.

Rich pulled a cigarette from his pack and propped it between his lips.

* * *

The ride to Marcus's house was a haze of red taillights in the
fog. Orange light shined through crystallized windows on Rich
and Uri making out in the backseat.

"Stop being gross," Marcus said, flicking the rearview mirror
up while swerving around cars on the icy streets.

The party started off with just twelve gay guys in the lush
two-story house, drinking and listening to a mix of techno and
assorted pop vomit. Over the next hour other mutual friends
arrived until more than thirty people, mostly guys, crowded
the living room, kitchen and patio. Colorful glass pipes were
passed around, and the den was soon enshrouded in a haze of
skunky smoke.

Rich and Uri got in on it. Uri was shy about smoking pot, but
Rich was eager for free social lubricant. He became increasingly
wild with each puff of weed and shot of liquor as the night went
on. He loosened up, lost his hoodie, lost his shirt, entered the free
tribal state he normally bottled up. The vulture wings on his bony
shoulder blades seemed to flap as he jumped around the party
talking to different circles of guys, telling the same stories about
each tattoo while scratching the top of his head childishly.

"You're having fun," Uri said to Rich as he bounced to a stop
in front of the kitchen counter full of liquor bottles.

Rich poured rum into Coke in a red cup and handed it to Uri.
"I didn't think being around gay guys would be fun, but they
seem to like me." He swigged from the rum. "I didn't even know
there was a gay crowd in this town."

Uri sipped from his cup and frowned against the rum, wiping
his lip. "Yeah, this is pretty much the gay illuminati of this town,
all concentrated in one house."

"You make it sound scary."

"Some of these guys have girlfriends, totally separate lives when they're not hanging with Marcus's crowd scoring drugs or fucking each other." Uri pointed out each guy in the crowd smoking in the living room. "Rugby player, student government senator, frat, frat, engaged, Christian frat, former gymnast."

"That's kind of shady."

"And they all hate me," Uri said.

"Why?"

Uri smiled and held up his camera. "Beautiful boys like them are naturally cam whores, but not when it's in my hands."

"You have a way of getting people's faces out there."

"After some bullshit a few months ago, I pretty much can't tag anyone, and my Facebook albums have to be private. Not all of them hate me." Uri shrugged. "Marcus and Jason like me, but they're out."

"So I guess I'm your outlet," Rich said.

"What do you mean?"

"I'm the one hot guy you can show everyone else."

"That's a rather high opinion of yourself."

"You've done a good job pumping my ego."

Uri kissed Rich's sternum, running his hands up his ribs to his collarbone. "Well, here's another. They're now all jealous of me and it feels like flying."

"You're stoned. The blog isn't enough validation?"

"Oh, right, those people. But I don't know those people. I don't care about anonymous people. It means nothing compared to this."

"You're out of your mind if you put value on what these people think."

Uri licked his lips and rubbed his temple. "I'm not. I'm not stoned."

Rich kissed Uri and glanced through his hair, spotting the jockish tanned guys who were stealing glances back at them.

Rich was a riddle, something quirky and unusual in the crowd of primped hairless jocks. They knew Rich wasn't a college student. They didn't know he was a high school dropout, but some, more sober, probably assumed it, based on his appearance.

Jason, the porn star whore, danced on a steel coffee table stripped down to his black briefs. Multicolored lights on the Christmas tree painted his body in reds, blues and greens. The jocks hollered and smacked his ass and pulled on the elastic band of his briefs, snapping it against his tan line.

"Most of these parties turn out this way," Uri said, falling back into Rich's torso in the kitchen archway. "Once enough of the prudes and two or three confused straight guys leave, the rest will land up naked, fucking each other, maybe right there in the living room."

Rich pulled his arms around Uri. "You're full of shit."

Uri laughed. "Okay, that's only happened once, and I wasn't even there when it did, but who knows."

Rich stumbled, adjusting his weight, pulling Uri closer, swaying him around in his arms and nuzzling his ear. "Would you join them?"

"No, I'm ugly," Uri said. "But I would sneak a few photos if I could."

"You're not ugly," Rich said kissing his ear. "You're my handsome Ukrainian boy."

"Don't try."

"You look like one of those young boyish Russian soldiers."

"The kind that sell their bodies for sex because they're poor?"

"If you want," Rich said.

In the living room, Jason continued to dance on the coffee table to thumping club music. A short, muscular, redhead rugby player named Colt pulled Jason's briefs down, exposing bright white skin and coarse trimmed pubes. Jason kept dancing, his soft cut dick and balls bouncing, meaty glutes flexing as he turned to show his ass. The redhead put Jason's dick in his mouth and sucked on it. Jason gyrated, unaffected. Some of the guys hooted, others leaned back and watched like they would in a strip club.

Rich grabbed Uri's camera from a step on the kitchen stairwell. "Holy shit, we gotta get this." He flipped it on.

"Wait, wait," Uri said, hushing him. "Turn the flash off or do movie mode."

Rich spun the wheel on the camera settings to movie mode. "This breed of closet jock must be documented." He aimed the lens at the debauchery.

Jason's cock swelled to seven inches from Colt's sloppy tonguing; he clutched the base of his dick and humped into the rugby player's lips.

Colt buried his nose in Jason's sculpted pubes, chin grinding the sometime porn star's hairless balls, freckled dimples folding as he gurgled down Jason's cock like a pro.

Uri grinned like an imp and snuck behind Rich, who held the camera at his side, halfway peeking through the archway of the kitchen. The kitchen lights were off, the darkness obscuring them from those in the sunken den. "On the rugby team Colt's nickname is Lips because he's got nice thick ones," Uri said. "If only they knew the use he got out of them."

"Maybe they will," Rich muttered, gently nudging the zoom on the camera. "I hate closet jocks."

A large number of shy prudes left the party as more guys lost their shirts and jeans and put their hands on each other until an intimate group of just eleven or twelve remained. Marcus, big and jolly and giggling, stayed on the sidelines, having no problem being host and witness to hot guys devouring each other in his den.

Colt, the rugby player, grew furious on Jason's cock, lips pounding down to the base. Jason groaned, the first utterance in his stoned haze, a feminine groan. Colt slid off Jason's cock and grabbed his ankles, where the black briefs bunched up. He yanked them hard and the dancing porn star flew onto his back, smashing down on the steel coffee table, glasses and cups rattling. Some of the guys laughed. Colt squatted and clawed Jason's tan pecs while devouring his cock. He grabbed Jason's thighs and thrust them in the air. He slid his tongue down Jason's cock and balls and buried it in his hairless, meaty ass. Jason let out a high-pitched squeal. The jock's tongue found no resistance and fucked deep into him, teeth grazing his sphincter. Jason grabbed Colt's hair, pulling his face harder into his ass. The rugby player reached up and smacked the hand away with a swipe of his forearm.

"Fuck!" Jason yelled, cradling his wrist.

Colt grunted with an underbite and wrapped his arms around Jason's tanned, waxed thighs and pulled him against his own hard body. He spat in his hand and polished his fat, uncut, six-inch cock. He squatted and shoved it into Jason's ass, bare.

"Oh, fuck!" Jason cried. "Fuck me," he moaned.

The muscled guys surrounding the coffee table fished their cocks out and jacked off over Jason. Colt pounded Jason's ass ruthlessly, his own asscheeks shaking with each slam. One of the guys shoved his cock between Jason's lips. The porn star sucked it expertly, as if he knew he was on camera.

Rich tried to keep Uri's camera steady in his hands. Uri was horny, so overwhelmed by the sight of the Grecian jock orgy that he couldn't stop himself from slipping his hands into Rich's jeans, reaching around to grab balls and cock. Rich faltered and set the camera on the counter, lens aimed into the living room scene of guys moaning, jacking and fucking.

"You wanna get fucked, too?" Rich spun around and gnawed on Uri's Adam's apple.

"Fuck, yes," Uri said.

Rich fished a lubricated condom from his pocket and dropped his jeans. He slipped the condom over his hard-on. Uri dropped his jeans and briefs and grabbed hold of the archway above his head. Rich squatted behind the shorter Uri, arching his cock up into his tight, hairless hole, pushing his cock in with his fist.

Uri squirmed in pain, ass fighting Rich's cock. Rich pressed the rest of the way in when Uri's ass gave way. He pounded him gently and slid his fingers up Uri's outstretched torso, fondling his nipples.

Uri panted and Rich's pelvis cupped his asscheeks. He watched guy after guy take turns fucking Jason up the ass and down his throat. One guy came across Jason's face, getting jizz in his eye. Another came across his nipples. A fully clothed jock licked it up in a long sloppy drag. Another beefy blond came up Jason's ass, cum spilling out the porn star's sphincter around the next invading cock pummeling the raw red hole.

Rich snuck his hand around Uri's hip, grabbing hold of his dick. He jacked Uri, fucking him up the ass with long slow strides, burying himself balls deep, sliding out to the tip then shoving balls deep again. His dangling sac nuzzled against Uri's. He bit the hair on Uri's neck, digging his lip ring in.

"Fuck. I'm not gonna last," Uri groaned as Rich's pelvis slapped his asscheeks and hand polished his cock, smearing precum all over his head and loose foreskin.

Jason jacked himself as a fifth guy pounded him and shoved his load into him. Guys dragged their nails across Jason's chest. A massive Pacific Islander jock with long braided hair slammed his orgasm into Jason and grabbed his feet and snaked his tongue between his toes.

Jason cried out, writhing, and his own cum splattered his neck to a chorus of male moaning.

Rich's hand fluttered on Uri's cock, fist pumping and sliding his foreskin. Uri humped back into Rich's rhythm and stifled his growl, spewing his load on the kitchen floor. Rich kept fucking, dragging his fingers up Uri's ribs to his nipples, nearly twisting them off as he got his rocks off inside him. He slid out, condom quarter-full with spunk.

The orgiastic men in the den wiped themselves up, lounged and passed a pipe, the room filling with a skunky haze again. None of them could see Uri and Rich as they dressed in the pitch-dark kitchen. Rich threw his used condom in the sink.

Uri grabbed his camera from the counter. The red light was still on, indicating it was recording. It was just nearing the limit of its memory card.

Uri shoved the camera into Rich's hoodie pocket and looked up into his eyes. Rich grinned downward, devilish canines over his lip. Uri silently laughed into the air, hopped, then pulled Rich down for a kiss.

They ran out the back door, through the backyard, out the gate, through the paved back alley of the wealthy neighborhood, until they made it to the street. Uri jumped around as Rich lit a cigarette.

Uri laughed, condensation billowing from his mouth into the freezing fog lit orange by the streetlights. "I can't believe you did that! I can't believe that happened!"

"Look what you've done," Rich said, stumbling in the middle of the street, puffing his cigarette. "You turned me into a voyeur."

Marcus lived a few blocks from Uri's house, and they walked home in the fog, nuzzling each other for warmth in the raw air.

"What do we do with this?" Uri asked as he scanned through the thirty-minute video recording on his computer. It was a sweaty, glistening, well-lit orgy of athletic bodies, topped with Rich and Uri's close panting and shadows.

Rich, naked and showered, blew smoke over Uri's hair, resting his chin on top of his head. He watched as Uri replayed one of the guys cumming on Jason's face, over and over.

"I don't know. Now that I'm sobering up, I think we should probably delete it. The gay illuminati will come for us."

"Fuck them. We could put it on our own XTube amateur page," Uri said. "Make loads of cash, then I could put it on my blog. Anything tagged *frat*, *athlete* or *amateur jock* automatically gets a shitload of views."

"How long do you think you could get away with that?" Rich asked.

"Long enough to get money."

Rich tapped his cigarette in a coffee mug, eyes on the ceiling, musing over the idea of being less impoverished. "But what do we do if people want more? People always want more," Rich said.

Uri unplugged the camera from the computer and pointed it at Rich.

Rich leaned back on the bed, letting the cigarette dangle from his bottom lip as it curled into a smirk. His wiry arms turned and flexed, blue feathers of his eagle tattoo on his left arm shimmering over damp skin and veins.

Uri winked into the camera's little viewfinder at the convex image of Rich's suddenly willing blue eyes, eyes fresh from the rush of exhibition, eyes now eager to be exhibited.

SEA MONSTERS

Matthew Lowe

We've been drinking all morning, Ash and me, feet up on the front porch. Neither of us has a job at the moment, so we tend to spend a lot of time out here, just loafing in deck chairs. Ash has only been with us a couple of weeks. I suppose we're still in the getting-to-know-you stages. Jamie, his boyfriend, is a friend of ours. When he came to take our spare room, Ash came too.

Ash is nice enough. He is certainly nice to look at, a man who carries his beauty with easy grace. He came up from the coast to be with Jamie and he's still got that warm holiday glow about him.

The weekend after they moved in, my boyfriend Michael filled the bathtub with ice, and we threw an impromptu housewarming party.

Jamie was keen to show Ash off. Like the proud curator of a museum's perfect piece of art, he clung to his discovery, only letting go of him when he needed to slip outside for a smoke, or return to the bathroom for a drink.

You could tell Jamie was thrilled by all the attention Ash was bringing him. He spent most of the evening fielding inquiries about his new beau. *When? Where? How big? How often?* But as the night wore on he began to look a little threatened. The same magnetism that had drawn him in drew others, too. They circled the happy couple like sharks at feeding time.

At the end of the night when we were collecting the empties and taking them out to the bin, Ash stopped and threw his arms around my neck.

"I'm glad I moved down here," he said. "I really like living with you guys." His breath was warm against my neck. I could feel the ripples of his firm body as he pressed against me.

"Lucky that Monday's bin day," I said.

Michael and Jamie have gone to work and Ash and I are in our usual spots on the porch. He's telling me about the time he spent working the trawlers on the Coffs Coast and I'm just listening, trying to remember if I saw him eat breakfast before he cracked his first beer.

"It was real hard work," he says, "Sometimes you'd get a seal up on deck. I tell you what, I don't care how cuddly they look on *World Around Us*, they're fuckin' vicious, those seals. Pretty much have to bash their heads in before you can get 'em back in the water."

I swig warm beer and wince.

"Well, you think about it...you're a seal...you get pulled up into the sky, and next thing you know you're on top of a mountain of fish. That's gotta be like seal heaven, right? Would you get back into the cold water?"

"S'pose not," I say. "Still, you must pull up all kinds of things out there."

"Oh, yeah. You get all sorts of shit in those nets: turtles, sharks...one time we caught a dolphin. That was real horrible. Big cow, she was. Fat as anything. Poor bitch must have been pregnant. Must have dragged her around behind us for hours because by the time we pulled her up she'd drowned."

Ash spits out his tongue like he's tasted something bad, then he leans forward to reach for a smoke. He plants his nose in the foil, draws a cigarette from the packet with his lips, leans back, cups his hands and lights up.

"One day we hauled up this Great White. Man, they can be real big bastards. This one wasn't though—maybe a meter... meter fifty...anyway it's thrashing around the deck, making all kinds of mess. So I get it into my head that I want its jaws— you know how people keep them shark jaws? Hang 'em up and stuff? Well, the boss says, 'If you can convince 'im to give 'em to you, they're yours.' But do you think that shark was gonna give 'em up without a fight? No fuckin' way! Took me three hours to kill it, and I was using everything I could—an oar, this big plank I found. In the end I had to pull out my fishing knife and slice through its skull, and all the while it's thrashing around having a go." Ash shook his head and took a swig. "Man, I wanted those jaws," he said. "Could have got into a lot of trouble for having them though. They're protected now, them sharks. Vicious buggers."

"So what happened?" I ask.

"Well, I cut them out and cleaned 'em up, and they were in my house down the coast for yonks."

"Where are they now?"

"Dunno...brother's probably..." Ash sucks on the last of his smoke and throws the used end into the flowerbed.

Halfway through the day we run out of beer, so the two of us wander up to the bottlo for a carton.

Ash says he's feeling generous, so he takes the carton to the counter. I don't think to ask how he'll pay for it. It's been six weeks since he moved in, and there's still no job to speak of. On the way home we take turns carrying the slab: Ash, with the box high above his head, and his short legs working hard to keep up; then me, carrying the carton across my arms, thongs slapping at the bitumen. We don't say much. I try not to look at him when it's his turn to carry, though the carton makes every muscle on him tense and quake.

Once we're home Ash wastes no time kicking off his shoes, mousing into the box and twisting the cap off a warm beer.

"Shit!" he curses, shaking the spray from his hands. "Should have known that'd happen."

He peels his T-shirt from his shoulders and tosses it behind him. And that's when I see the octopus, a sinister creature peering at me like a shadowy trick of the afternoon sun, its dark arms encircling his shoulder.

"You're not lying," I say. "You're a real fisherman—tatts and all."

"Oh, that? That was my mate's brother. He was training to be a tattoo artist. They always need skin to draw on, them guys. Got it free, 'cause I was the guinea pig, but it was meant to be twice as big."

I watch him turn his arm over, tracing a wayward tentacle along his tight tricep.

"So, why'd you give up the trawlers?" I ask when we're settled back into our spots on the porch.

"Dunno," he says. "Got tired of it, I guess. Money was good, I'll give you that. But there's never anywhere to spend it out at sea, is there? And you can be out there for weeks. Pretty scary when you think about it. So far from land…"

We're silent for a while. I watch as Ash starts picking the

label from his stubbie. I can't take my eyes off that animal. It sits on his shoulder, waiting.

"One time, when we were out in open water, I got this pain. I didn't know what it was for a while, but then it started getting real bad, real quick. We were miles from the coast and some of the other guys were releasing the trawls, and here I am in the bottom of the cabin, doubled over, feeling about as useful as tits on a bull. I couldn't move or eat or spew. And man, did it cane! I've never known pain like it. 'Ventually I made that much noise that the others started talking about turning back. And then I passed out."

"Geez! What happened?"

"Well, they turned back. And just as well they did! My appendix had burst. I ended up in hospital for two weeks. Tell you what though, if we'd been out a bit further or we'd come back a bit later I mightn't have been so lucky. I mightn't have been here telling you 'bout it. 'Course the boss would've had us out for longer if he could have. Bosses are the greediest bastards going. When we got back to port, all he wanted to know was why we hadn't brought back a bigger catch. More worried about the wasted fuel than my wasted appendix... That did me for the trawlers for a while. I never went out again after that. I'll show you the scar," he said, lowering the top of his shorts just enough to reveal the wide base of his dick.

"Pretty gnarly scar, huh? Ten stitches."

At about four thirty Jamie comes home from work. "What have you two been up to all day?" he calls, walking up the path. "Did you look for a job?"

"Thought about it," Ash says.

"You thought about it? Did you look?"

"Yeah. What do you think I do all day?" Ash shoots back.

They cross the doormat and the flyscreen swings back noisily.

I wait for Michael, but the mozzies beat him home so I end up shifting from the porch to the couch.

Under the yellow glow of *The Simpsons*, I can hear them moving around the kitchen, Ash and Jamie, with their complicated cooking.

"When?" Jamie says.

"I dunno...tomorrow..."

"That's what you told me yesterday, Ash. I want to know that you're actually going to go."

"Hey, I said I would. What more do you want?"

"I want you to go. Tomorrow. Instead of just talking about it."

"Oh, come on, Jay! You nag like a bitch. If I wanted to be with a woman I would."

There's silence in the kitchen for a while. Then as the saucepans begin to bubble you can hear them at it again, arguing in hushed tones, guilting each other with lists of everything they've given up to be together.

That night I lay awake thinking of our strange new housemate, his seafaring tales and his poster-boy good looks. How charming and how alarming he seems to me, this charismatic stranger in the room at the end of the hall.

Ash stands on the balcony, the weary sun fading behind him, his brown eyes dancing in the twilight. His smile seems as real in my dreams as it had that afternoon, when he stood before me, bare-chested and beautiful, his brown arms folded, barring his perfect body.

In the heat of the afternoon my beer drools like melting ice cream, its sweat running down my hand, dripping and disap-

pearing on the scorched cement. I cross to the railing where he
sits sunning himself. He raises a hand to shield his eyes, and I seize
my chance, driving the cold heel of my stubbie into his side.

"Ah, you dirty bastard!" he yelps, leaping high into the air.
"You can be a real cunt, you know?"

He flicks the beer from his belly, stroking the warmth back
into his ribs. Suddenly, he launches himself toward me, his
shoulder connecting with my stomach, sending me backward.

"Not so tough now, huh?" he says, pulling me into a clinch.
He has me from behind, his arms locked around mine, his biceps
tense and firm, hugging my chest. I twist my body so that I'm
facing him, pushing off on my elbows till his fingers give way at
my back. For a second I fall free, then he latches on to me again.
His shoulders slacken and tighten and that dark octopus looms
in, spreading its tentacles, swiping the air.

"Ash, let go," I say, "You're hurting me. I'm not kidding."

He untenses his grip. I'm exhausted and winded. I start
coughing, then I start laughing. His arms are still around me.
His eyes move over my face.

"I need another beer," I say, breaking away.

"You can have the rest of mine. You spilled enough of it on
me."

He kneels and picks up the stubbie.

"Here," he says, holding the bottle high above my head.

"You wouldn't," I say.

"Oh, no?"

His fingers tighten around my wrists. The bottle teeters above
dangerously. I shrink to my knees, flicking my arms in all direc-
tions to break free of his grip. Suddenly his fingers burst apart
like the broken ends of an elastic band and I'm tumbling backward, hurtling toward the tiles. There is a thump of water and
a rush of bubbles. Curtains close on the sky above me, on Ash

and his outstretched hand. I plummet into darkness and in that one final gasp of light, I can see the creature moving over him, black arms like mariners' knots all hitched and sheep-shanked and alive.

"What is it? What's happened?" Michael says. He's sitting up in bed next to me, his eyes searching the darkness furiously. There'd been a great thunderclap, or perhaps a slammed door.

He swings his legs to the floor, and the bed sways back like a boat in the breeze. There are angry voices in the kitchen. The lamp on the bedside table is switched on suddenly. And I lie back and close my eyes, my mind still dizzy with sea monsters.

PALOMINO

Dale Chase

Before I caught sight of the boy I never considered much beyond the next bank job. Been outlawing since fourteen, seen many a man killed and done a stretch in Yuma Prison which adds up to a hard life, but I am not one to complain as sometimes I am able to help others less fortunate.

Harlan Crawford and me run the Crawford gang, which is down to just four now that we lost Neely in the Medford job. Deputy shot him dead outside the bank, and it was a hard loss as Neely had a wife and kiddies in Nevada.

It's Harlan who wants a new man, and so he asked Abel Trice to join up as Abel is strong, no nonsense and a good shot, but Abel said we had to take his brother Jesse, too. And Harlan agreed, sight unseen. Then in they ride to our hideout on the Coote ranch and Jesse is but a boy. And I am lost to him because there is no word but beautiful.

He doesn't look like Abel who is red haired, freckled, pink skinned. Jesse looks more half-breed but wears it well, and maybe it's the mix of light and dark that has produced such a fine creature. He is shy, lets his brother speak, and I do likewise, allow Harlan to set things up among us. But I can't stop eyeing the kid because I've seen nothing like him, not ever. A woman might have such beauty but a man?

Abel, who is twenty-six, says the kid is nineteen, which I find difficult to believe as he seems such a boy. No beard I can detect, smooth skin of a golden hue, palomino if he was horseflesh. His eyes give away his native side, black like his hair and eyebrows. His cheekbones are strong, jaw likewise, and he seems better put together than the rest of us.

He catches me looking and I jump into the conversation, startled at being caught. "Train next, we're thinking," I say and Abel nods, says he did one train job but the marshals were on board, and they got no money and lost two men. "Anymore you need somebody inside," he adds, at which Harlan fairly beams.

"We got us a station agent," he says, and the kid listens, forgets about me so I steal a sideways glance because I can't resist. Part of me is asking what in God's hell is happening but the rest, including my dick, don't care.

The boy's pink mouth is full lipped like a woman's. I consider how those lips might feel on my cock, then force myself back to the conversation.

The cabin we inhabit on the Coote ranch is some distance from the main house where Merle Coote and wife reside. Merle allows us the place as we keep him supplied with stolen horses and money. We are careful never to be tracked there. After a job we hole up at Moncton Canyon or some such out of the way spot until there is no posse about. Then we come back to the ranch.

The cabin sits in a cottonwood grove alongside a decent stream and is a fine place to rest up between jobs. Town is not too far and we are known to spend our loot there, sometimes

too quickly at the gambling tables. I know no other life, and
now as I see Jesse, the boy, about to take it up, I wonder if he'll
be like me, ruined for honest work.

Abel says something that makes Jesse laugh, and I see a wide
smile, good teeth. The ache in me is familiar below the belt but
not so above. My life has left little room for matters of the heart,
but that organ seems affected now as much as the one in my
pants, although something also seems lodged in my gut. This is
not the usual way, like with Harlan, where we come upon one
another and have us a fuck.

I find myself welcoming the feeling Jesse brings, and I can't
take my eyes off him. My hands itch to get at him, not so much
to fuck as to run my fingers over that golden skin, to pull away
the clothes and pet him. As his smile fades and his mouth closes,
I think how it would be to have mine upon his. The urge is
strong to do that, but I never kissed no man, no woman neither.
Harlan and me don't do such things, don't pet one another, just
bare the necessities and do it.

Two weeks have passed since the Medford job, and much of
our money is gone. Some we gave to the Wainwright family who
were down on their luck and about to starve, Sam Wainwright
taken sick, wife nowhere to turn and three kiddies to feed. We
bought clothes and food, which was most welcome. Much of the
rest went to card games in town. Now Merle says we need to
bring him some horses, so before we rob any bank or train we
have that to do.

Jesse and Abel take bunks in the cabin, Abel in Neely's,
which don't seem to bother him. I make it a point to be inside
because I crave sight of the kid and sure enough, he strips off
his shirt. This all but takes my breath away, and I bring myself
to the table while stealing looks at a sturdy frame and more of
that palomino skin. He's well developed for such a young man,

hard work in his past. His tits are more brown than pink which excites me as it's more of that mix. No hair on him, smooth all over, and I think of my tongue on him, licking his places, and this gets me to what he has in his pants, which causes me to flee the cabin so I don't make a fool of myself.

I walk down to the stream where I attempt calm, but the urge is upon me and I give it free rein, think of Jesse naked, black patch of hair between his legs and a fresh young cock. My own is stiff and when Harlan joins me beside the water and says he thinks we've done good with the new men, I pull him into the trees and fuck him hard and quick.

Merle's wife Sarah gives us supper up to the house, and Jesse eats like a starving man. I keep my head down while the others talk about where to find horses to steal, when to do the job. Jesse is directly across from me, and I look up now and again to see him because he is unlike the rest of us who are worn and ragged with rough beards and coarse skin parched by outdoor life. Jesse looks just born, set upon this earth whole and beautiful. Thinking on this causes the ache to take me over, and I start to worry others can feel the heat, because Jesse looks over at me and holds his eyes to mine like he knows I'm captive to him. Then he smiles a little and goes back to his stew, and I am left struck not only by his attentions but by the thought that he is no outlaw.

I know there is a world beyond the one familiar to me, big cities like New York and San Francisco, and I think that's where Jesse belongs, dressed up among others who lead honorable lives and have no idea what it is to be on the run. But I have to stop myself thinking such things because the here and now is that he is part of our gang, so the most I can do is keep him from making a mistake and getting shot.

Abel don't pay much attention to the kid. After supper they

don't spend time together, Abel drinking whiskey with Vern
Lockhart and Bob Fisher who are the rest of our gang. Jesse
climbs into his bunk with some paper he brought along, some
sort of picture I'd venture. Looking at it, he don't seem to care
where he is, like the paper takes him away from us, and it makes
me want to see what he sees, so I get up from the table as if to
stretch, wander over near to him and look down. He can't help
but know I'm there beside him, and I like that he makes no move
to hide his picture. I find myself greatly relieved it's no girl but
is instead a rough pencil drawing of house and barn, corral,
fields beyond. And I wonder if he made this and if it might be
the place he and Abel come from, and my heart presses on me
terrible, like it could push out of my chest, because he is such a
boy, holding onto what likely is gone, otherwise he wouldn't be
here with Abel looking to outlaw.

"You draw that?" I ask and he nods. "Home?" I ask and
again the nod, and I see he don't want to talk about it, but I
want to keep on. "You draw anything else?"

"Sometimes," he says in near a whisper, which makes it feel
like we're talking secret.

"Other places or can you draw people, too?"

"Been known to. Only kept this one."

He don't sound sad about this, only resigned, and I wonder
what all has been left in that house and why his brother is making
him become one of us. But I can't say that here, and it fills up in
me, this wanting him but also wanting for him. So I back off, go
outside for a smoke.

"Why'd Abel bring the kid?" I ask Harlan when he joins me.

"Folks took sick and died so Abel went to look after him."

"This ain't no looking after."

Harlan don't say anything more and I fear he, by way of
knowing me, can see I'm all churned up by the boy. "Jesse's

old enough to find work and make his own way," I offer.

"You want him out of the gang?"

"Not saying that, just he doesn't seem outlaw material."

"Who in hell is?" Harlan laughs. "You raised up to rob banks? Christamighty, Frank, none of us chose it. Likely Abel didn't neither, and Jesse is old enough to have a say, and it appears he ain't said no."

"I suppose."

"Why's this after you?"

I pass a few seconds thinking to keep my secret but surely Harlan can see the beauty before us. And before I can rein myself in, I'm telling it. "Jesse is a beauty. Don't you see that? I never seen such beauty in a man, skin all golden and dark eyes and pink lips, almost a woman's mouth."

My prick gets hard from such talk but it's my middle that feels good saying it out loud.

"You looking to fuck him?" Harlan asks.

"It ain't all about fucking."

"Hell it ain't," he growls and he shoves a hand down to my crotch. When he pulls me into the barn I don't resist and when he fucks me standing I think on the kid and how he'll bend like this, feel my prick going at him like Harlan's at me.

I don't come while he's at it, so soon as he's emptied and pulled out I turn and push him into the hay, then get my dick into him, but all the while I'm thinking on the kid.

"You don't need to fuck no kid," Harlan says as we lie in the hay after. "You got all you can handle right here."

"Yep," I say, though I know better. And I realize then, in a moment similar to the one when I killed a man at fourteen, that my life is changing, and I may one day have to shoot Harlan Crawford. I also see how the Crawford gang might not be the only way ahead. This excites me while at the same time brings a dread cause I don't want to kill Harlan, but he has laid down a line I have already, in mind at least, crossed.

I don't sleep much that night. I listen to snores and to a hand working a prick, knowing it's Jesse, and I get a hand onto mine to share in the pleasure.

Next day all six of us ride some distance to steal horses belonging to Enoch Murphy. Vern brought word that Murphy had acquired a small herd and was coming down from Wyoming, which made them easy pickin's as they had but three men. Our plan is to pull the job around sunset when they've settled in for the night. Vern figures them near Backtrack Canyon, so we head there after one of Sarah Coote's good breakfasts.

Abel and Jesse ride together much of the way, same as me and Harlan, and I am further taken by the boy astride his horse. It's a little brown and white paint, more Indian pony, which adds to his mix. I think how he'd look in buckskin pants and moccasins, shirtless, face painted. He rides like he's born to it, and I think on those legs around me while my dick is in him.

Jesse is told to stick by Abel, just follow what he does. Near dark we find the herd tucked into the canyon. Harlan and me approach from the east, snaking down the canyon wall to surprise the men in their camp while Abel and the others appear up front. Though I've done this about a hundred times before, it seems new and I watch Jesse, who I find watching me.

Murphy's men make a mistake by putting up a fight, so we shoot two and the other gives up. We take their horses along with the herd and drive them halfway to Merle's before we make camp. We keep watch on the herd in shifts, and when I volunteer so does Jesse. As the others settle at the campfire, we are left to guard the perimeter.

The moon has seen fit to provide us its whole self, casting a blue light over the prairie. Astride our horses, we should ride separately but neither makes an effort toward this. Fortunately the stock remains quiet, so we just keep an eye out.

"How's it feel?" I ask him.

"What?"

"Being an outlaw—because you are one now."

"Don't know," he says, not looking at me. The light keeps half of him in dark, the other half that blue color, and I see his lips parted as if words are there but he can't get to them. The ache in me grows strong.

"This your idea or Abel's?" I ask.

He shrugs and I see he don't much care what he is or where.

"Any way I can help?" I ask.

He turns to me and maybe its night come upon us or maybe just me pushing my desire onto him, but he don't look sweet no more. He looks like some hungry wolf cub, and he smiles a crooked sort of thing, a leer maybe. Not a word is needed.

I get off my horse, pull him from his, and we stand between them as I take hold of this creature who has gotten inside me. "I mean to have you," I tell him as I pull him to me. His mouth opens like he's thirsty, and I see a bit of tongue which drives me near insane so I do it, put my mouth to his, tongue to his, and, lordy, how we grind against one another as we taste and kiss and lick.

We are at the back of the herd, well out of sight, and so I open my pants, get out my hard prick. Jesse drops his drawers and turns, presents me his bottom, and there in the moonlight between the horses I fuck him.

I want to howl with pleasure. As I shove into him he rocks back at me and tells me to fuck him. Over and over he says it, and we set us up a motion I'd have to call a galloping fuck, rocking back and forth as I drive my thing up him. But it's too much, and my juice boils in my balls, and I start to come, spurting my stuff into him and telling him I'll fuck him to kingdom come every day from now on. I keep this up till I am empty, but even then I don't want to let him go. I pull him back against me, which causes me to slip out of him, but I rub the whole of him, reach around for his cock, which is soft, so he must have let go while I was in him.

Then I turn him to me, and I have me a real kiss. Not urgent, just take my time with my lips on his and he responds in kind, holding on to me, nether regions together.

The horses stir as they smell the sex. "We keep on, they'll stampede," I finally say and Jesse chuckles, and I like making him happy.

"I want to keep on with you," I add. "You're like no other man, ever."

"What about Harlan?"

Here I close my pants and he does likewise. "Harlan and me just fuck," I say. "It's different with you."

He nods and we mount up, walk the perimeter as silent as the horses.

I would have thought fucking the kid might ease me but it's the opposite. It fans the flame and also douses that with Harlan, so the next time he gets at me I let him do it but make no effort to get into him. And he takes note.

"You off your feed?" he asks as he tucks his prick into his pants. We're in Merle's barn and my dick hasn't gotten stiff.

"Guess so," I say.

He leaves it at that, and I am grateful because since we stole the horses a week ago, Jesse and me have gotten up to all manner of things, and I can't believe Harlan don't know.

Every time the boy goes off alone I find a way to follow, and I am good at covering my tracks. I make sure Harlan is occupied drinking whiskey up at Merle's or some such. I'll go to check the horses and pull Jesse into the barn. And he's as much in need as me, throwing off his clothes and pointing his stiff prick at me, asking me to suck the come out of him which I do, swallowing his stuff, which riles me so I ram my cock into him harder than usual. And I get my fingers into his bottom and God help me, my tongue.

One time I'm sucking his prick, and he starts saying how he wants me to lick his backside, and I am surprised by this as I never done such a thing, nor has Harlan that I know of. It sounds filthy which makes me want it, so once he's come in my throat he turns, spreads his buttocks and says to lick his crack, so I do it, get my face down there where it don't belong, and I run my tongue up the split between bottom halves. Then I find the center, the hole where my dick goes. Jesse is squirming, says to get into him, he wants my tongue to fuck him, and so I plaster my mouth onto him and shove in. He moans with pleasure and I taste his bitterness, which riles me all the more because it's real filth and don't that go with a fuck?

As I do this I can't help but get a hand on my prick, start working myself, and soon I am tongue fucking and coming, which is one more thing Jesse has brought me. Since I took up with him I have known all manner of nasty pleasure, which is surprising as he looks so innocent.

Once I've come I pull off, wipe my mouth on my sleeve, but Jesse pulls me up to get his mouth on mine and his tongue goes in, sucking mine, and he starts grinding against me, never mind he just came. His young cock is up again and I squeeze his buttocks, put a finger into him, and he starts to come again.

One time he bathes in the stream and I go down there and get into the water with him, so we're both naked. It's a hot day; Harlan has gone to town with Vern and Bob, and Abel is sleeping in his bunk. Merle and Sarah and even the kiddies are quiet up to the house. The place seems asleep, so we share the water where it's too shallow for much cover but enough to wash and cool in. And we do wash and we do cool ourselves like any two men might, but our pricks are up, so I sit in the water and pull Jesse onto my lap, put my dick up him, and he rides me awhile, making it an easy fuck while I reach around and rub his tits until they are hard, then drop a hand down to play with his cock. Soon he bucks and spurts, but he keeps astride me, and I manage a good long fuck before my juice rises, and I come into him.

When he gets off of me he slides around in the water and lays on me, kissing. He is good at using his mouth, and we kiss for some time, and then he slides down, nips at my tits, licks my belly, then gets down to my prick, which lies heavy and spent on my thigh. And he gets his lips onto it, sucks and pulls, takes it into his mouth and works until it starts to stiffen. It makes me want to fuck him again, but he won't let go and soon I can't help myself, and I am coming into his mouth and watching as he swallows what I give. It's at this moment that I know we are one and nothing must be allowed to come between us. I had no life before Jesse, but now I see more life than I could ever imagine, and once he finishes sucking my cock, I tell him this. He is my life. I want no other.

Here I wrap my arms around him, and we lie in the cool water not trying to pleasure one another, no hard dicks or nothing, just holding on, which I never done with no man, and I find a contentment that is new. Thinking back I cannot recall ever being this much at peace, and we lie in the water in the sun and I look down at his golden skin speckled with drops, glistening like some jewel, and I look at his young prick finally at rest there below that black patch and think how I had it in my mouth and will again, how the whole of him is mine. I squeeze him tighter as these thoughts warm me.

Later on we help Merle with branding horses. All the gang work the stock and do chores around the ranch, which is only fair as Merle takes a chance having outlaws living on his spread. Harlan and me work side by side like nothing is different, and I find I want to tell him things have changed but have no words for such. And as we work I decide he likely knows already because he hasn't fucked me or asked for it now for some days. He goes into town on his own, which he never did much before, so I'm wondering if he's found someone else to fuck, and I hope he has.

Evenings after supper we plan our next holdup. We put off robbing a train because Abel says he knows of a bank ripe for the pickin'. Harville, a town some hundred miles north, has two banks, one at each end of town, and his gang had been scouting one for some time, so he knows it well; how there's two tellers and at noon time just one. It's the smaller bank and it becomes our target. Abel says he knows miners keep their money there, and it is said to be well stocked with cash and gold. We decide to do the job our usual way, which is to have two men and fresh horses stationed halfway there so we can outrun a posse, which we have done many a time. Vern and Bob will do this as Abel says he wants Jesse with him. So we six set out for the long ride north. Early that morning I fuck Jesse good and hard, knowing we might not get much for a few days.

Supplies are laid in at the cabin in Moncton Canyon, and the six of us then ride on north. Jesse wears a determined look, hat pulled low, mouth set. I enjoy the sight of him astride his paint, recall licking his bottom and how he likes to spread his cheeks and beg me to get in back there. He is a truly remarkable creature, and I must work to keep him safe. I'd wanted to suggest he stay with the horses halfway but saw that Abel would never have such a thing. The older brother seems bent on turning Jesse bad.

Harlan rides beside me and I feel the pull of the two men, one who has my attentions and who I crave night and day, the other who has my history and who has by way of his gun kept me safe. Harlan is a good man; I fault him for nothing, and it's none of his doing that he has lost me to the boy. God or nature or maybe just a man and his desire are at work. I'd like to tell him, but we don't talk on such things, so he is left on his own. But I'm sure he knows. I admire that he has made no changes toward me other than not fucking. He is strong in many ways.

We camp at the halfway point, which is some craggy rocks grown high up out of the plain. They give a break from the wind as they provide cover from one direction so a man can't be caught unawares. They also provide a place where Jesse and me can get out our dicks and suck one another, which we do under cover of night. There is just no keeping off.

Next day we ride on to Harville, where we act like any cowboys in off the range. We split up, some to stroll about and have a smoke, others to take a drink in the saloon. Around noon we work our way toward the bank. The horses were left there when we rode in, and we now put Jesse outside with them while we three, Harlan, Abel and me, enter the bank. One teller is at work with a customer and another man waits his turn.

We pull down our masks soon as we're inside, and Harlan calls out, "Throw up your hands!" which all do. Soon he is behind the counter stuffing money and gold into sacks that he hands over to Abel and me. All goes perfectly and once we have what we want, we back out slowly keeping guns drawn.

Outside we head toward the horses, Jesse now astride his paint. I sling a sack of loot up to him and climb into my saddle while Abel and Harlan also mount up. But as they take their places I hear someone shout, "Stop!" and gunshots cut through the air. I turn to see Harlan arch, head thrown back, for he has been hit from behind. I shoot a man holding a rifle, a man with a badge. As he falls so does Harlan, and I want to climb down and get my man, bring him with us, but Abel calls out, "Let's go!" and Harlan ain't moving, and I know he's dead but still I can't leave.

"He's dead, Frank, come on!" Abel shouts, and I know he's right and I see other men with guns running toward us, so I spur my horse and we ride out full gallop leaving Harlan there shot dead on the ground.

We don't let up because we know a posse is forming and will soon be on our heels. It's also good for me to ride hard because if I slow down I will know only torment and that I cannot bear. I don't look to Jesse, I don't look to nobody. I just ride for all get out.

By the time we reach the fresh horses, ours are worn out and we know those of the posse will be likewise, and thus our escape is made. Vern and Bob join us and we ride on to Moncton Canyon, which we reach next day. By then nobody is after us and we are safe with our money, but still we spend two days in the canyon to let the dust settle on the robbery.

Abel steps in to count the money. Harlan always did that, and I have no complaint that Abel takes over as he is much like Harlan, strong in that way, man of action and born leader I suppose. I cannot bear to be inside the cabin, cannot stand the company of others, even Jesse. I take my bedroll up the canyon, climbing to an outcropping I know, and there I lie in pain like I have never known before.

Harlan near crushes me with his weight as I recall everything about him, how we first met up in Tombstone in a saloon brawl that led us to partner and to fuck something fierce. After that we stuck together, and when we discovered we'd both killed men early in life and taken the outlaw path, we formed our gang.

That was six years ago, so all that time we was partners. Looked out for one another, saved each other more than once, had us some fights and dustups but usually fucked our way out of them. And now he's dead and I cannot bring myself to think of what they will do to him, how he likely will have no decent burial.

I think then on how it felt to fuck him, his powerful body giving way to my prick. Or how it felt for him to get into me, how I liked his roughness, big cock going in like an angry snake, causing me all manner of pleasure. We knew one another. We might not have said so, but we had something and now it is gone. And having Jesse there don't help at all, maybe makes it worse.

Next day, Jesse comes up to my spot with some food, says he respects my need to be alone, but I should eat something. He says he's sorry I lost Harlan, knows he was a big part of my life. I choke down some grub but hardly taste it and as for the kid, I just want him gone. Ain't no beauty no more; ain't no nothing.

Jesse retreats and I am grateful he understands my loss, which leads me to think on his recent loss, his ma and pa taken sick and dying. So he lives with his pain, and now I'll live with mine, and don't that beat all.

When I have grieved enough to face the men, I come down off my perch and join them. They have split up the money and my share waits for me. It's around twelve hundred dollars. Abel says they been talking about the gang without Harlan.

"We can keep on as before," he says. "You and me, Frank, we can run this outfit just fine, no disrespect to Harlan. What do you say?"

We are out front of the cabin as it is afternoon and the day is warm. Some sit in chairs, some stand. I look to Jesse who sprawls in his chair. He is hatless, black hair shiny in the light, skin golden, and I think how I want to pet him. He sees me looking and he runs his tongue over his lips then smiles, and my tongue escapes my mouth to also display itself.

"I'm leaving," I say to them all, having decided just that second. "Done with outlaw life. Maybe head to California, get me a spread or dig for gold. Maybe just play cards in San Francisco awhile, but I don't want no more robbing and killing."

Abel nods. "Fair enough. Boys, we can still keep on," he says to the others, and Vern and Bob say they're in. Abel don't look to Jesse, like the kid has no say, so Jesse gets out of his chair, comes over to his brother.

"I'm no outlaw, Abel, so count me out," he says. "I'll go with Frank, if he'll allow it."

Until then I hadn't thought of him and me together. That was done in by Harlan's death, everything gone by way of gunshot. But now something in me sparks, and I look to the kid who waits for my answer. He holds hat in hand like a gentleman caller and almost smiles because he knows he's already inside me, that I just covered him over for a time with my grief.

"You are welcome to join me," I say, and this breaks something in me and I want to laugh and cry at the same time, such is the well of feelings. Jesse comes over to me and we stand together. "You okay with this?" I ask Abel.

The big redhead eyes the two of us, and I see he is disappointed. He takes his time before he speaks, then says it's okay with him. "Would have liked to keep you with me," he tells Jesse, "but I respect you're a grown man and can make your own way. Knowing Frank here will keep an eye on you will allow me to rest easy."

"I'll keep him out of trouble," I say to Abel. "Myself, too," I add, which lightens things.

We plan to ride back to Merle's in the morning, which gives us a last night in the canyon. Heat lingers, so Jesse and me climb up to the outcropping with our bedrolls, make us a bed, then strip naked and lie together. And I pet him all over as the light dies away, kiss his lips. We are slow to get to the rest. His prick is hard from the first, but I don't hurry to it and he chuckles as my fingers play in the hair down there, then get under to cup his balls. Finally he moans, so I turn him onto his side and put my prick into him, and there we lie, me and my beautiful palomino boy.

A LITTLE
NIGHT MUSIC

Tom Mendicino

The charms of Prague are fading as the temperature plunges to minus six centigrade. My face is raw and chapped, my toes are numb in my boots, and a polar fleece vest and Carolina Tar Heels hoodie are poor insulation against the bitter winds whipping through the sloping streets of the Hradcany district. I stomp my feet, trying to generate enough body heat to survive as I wait for the night tram to roll down Keplerova. It arrives after an eternity, at least twenty minutes, its bright electric lights and a crush of bodies promising a haven from the cold. But when the doors close behind me, I'm trapped in an overheated, humid prison that reeks of stale Pilsner and body odor. A small dog—or maybe a large rat—scampers across my feet. I grab a pole, steadying myself before I topple into a filthy Rasputin muttering obscenities through his black teeth. The tram grinds to a halt, and one group of drunk students trying to disembark elbows and jostles another group trying to board. The hollow-eyed blonde next to me squeezes a ripe pimple on her forearm. Empty beer bottles roll under the seats as the tram lurches toward my stop at the doors of the department store, Tesco, the end of the line.

The brittle air is a tonic. One block ahead, on a narrow street that curves around the stone walls of an ancient church, is my refuge from the inhospitable Czech night. The boy at the reception desk takes my crown notes and asks in ungrammatical English if I want a locker or a cabin. The changing room where I peel off my clothes is spotless. I wrap a towel around my waist and slip my feet into a pair of clunky rubber shower shoes that I quickly shed after tripping on the stairs to the wet area. I hurry across the cold tile floor in my bare feet, enter the steam room and grope my way through a meandering maze, drawn toward the shadows lurking in the wet nooks and crannies and the promise of slick, wet skin. A hand reaches out and strokes my chest. My suitor, a middle-aged German businessman looking for quick orgasm after a long night of drinking, pushes me against the wall and grabs between my legs. I brush him aside and hurry away, slipping on a patch of liquid slicker than mere water. I take a long, hot shower. My clipped American penis is unimpressive compared to the flaccid uncut European cocks of the men lingering under the showerheads. There's a beauty swinging between the legs of the Cossack soaping his armpits; it's as thick as naval rope with a spotted mushroom head. I wonder what it looks like hard and ready for action. Only one way to find out. The fucking son of a bitch brushes my hand away. Cocksucker. Who the hell is he to be so choosy, with his receding hairline and double chin? I knot my towel around my waist and go in search of a wet mouth and a willing hole.

It sounds like a day at the zoo in this place: grunts, groans, guttural noises. *Put your cock in my mouth*, an Englishman begs as I hurry past his cabin. *Sorry, Lord Brideshead, nothing personal.* Everyone who wants me isn't my type, and no one I

want is interested. Coming to Prague was a mistake. The guide-
books promised a nonstop orgy (at an hourly rate if all else
failed), the perfect antidote for being dumped via email by my
transatlantic partner of seven years back in DC, who informed
me that absence did not make the heart grow fonder and that
he'd met the love of his life, a twenty-four-year-old White House
intern with a full head of hair and a virgin ass. Discouraged,
disheartened, disgusted, I convince myself to make one more
round through the bathhouse. If nothing more promising—or
willing—materializes, I'll drop off my key and my towel and
splurge on a cab. Better to be held hostage by the extortionist
Prague taxi mafia than suffer another adventure on the night
tram back to my hotel.

The door to Room 41 is ajar, inviting any curious hand to
open it. A pot-bellied bear mounting an eager cub is willing to
share his bounty, but frowns when I ask for a condom. I shrug
and step back into the hall, resigned to the night ending in frustration.

"Hello."

I turn and stare into the face of an angel sprawled across the
mattress of his brightly lit cubicle. I look to my left, then my
right, thinking he must be speaking to someone better looking,
more ripped and chiseled, than me. He strokes his long brown
penis and offers a blazing smile. I take a tentative step forward,
crossing the threshold of his room, still expecting him to shake
his head no when, after getting a better look, he realizes he's
made a mistake. But he spreads his legs and cups his round balls
in his hand, tugging at his scrotum.

"You like?"

"You speak English?" I ask, confirming the obvious.

"Yes. Of course. Come in. Please."

He tosses aside my towel and takes my cock in his mouth.

His tongue teases me to a full erection, then he slides his lips up and down the shaft, nibbling on the head.

"Is it nice for you?" he asks, his blue eyes twinkling, confident in his skill.

"Oh, yes."

"Please. Close the door."

I wedge my body against his on the narrow mattress. He throws his leg over my hip and grinds his cock against my belly.

"Will you be happy to fuck me now?" he asks.

His ass is already slick with lube. He watches with almost clinical interest as I roll a rubber over my hard-on.

"It is good. I am safe, too," he says before pressing his open mouth against mine and plunging his tongue deep into my throat.

A sweet, fleeting romance with this blue-eyed boy would be nice, twenty or thirty minutes of gentle touching and soulful glances ending in a passionate climax. But his body language says he wants to get straight down to business. He flips on his back and raises his legs, grabbing my hips and pulling me close enough for the head of my cock to tease his puckered hole.

"You will fuck me good?" he asks, less a question than a command to drive my pole deep inside his ass. I slip inside him easily and he thrashes against the mattress, challenging me to pump him harder, faster. He's not the shy, quiet type; pleasure is an experience to be shared at full volume, with grunts and moans and harsh, blunt syllables that need no translation. I shoot quickly and my penis shrivels in a condom full of wet semen. He bites his lower lip and frowns, obviously expecting better from a broad-shouldered, hairy-chested American. But disappointment is fleeting and he flashes a toothy smile. The boy is clearly an optimist.

"Let's have a cigarette. Then you fuck me again."

I haven't smoked in years and almost decline then decide to test whether tobacco is as seductive as it is in my fond memories. The first puff makes me light-headed, inexplicably happy. I cough and flop beside his lean, smooth body.

"We will rest," he says, squeezing my limp, sticky penis.

It's pleasant lingering here, basking in the heat pouring off his body for a few brief moments before it's time to brave the bitter cold. I fold my arm under his neck and he cuddles against my chest, drawing circles around my nipples with his long, tapered forefinger.

"Where are you from?"

"I'm an American."

"New York?"

I've lived abroad long enough to know that most Europeans believe that the entire population of the United States resides in California or the isle of Manhattan—except for Mickey Mouse, who lives in Orlando.

"Washington," I say.

"Ah," he says, intrigued by fantasies of proximity to prominent names in the international press. "Do you know the Clintons?"

I laugh at the presumption then admit I have, on occasion, been introduced to the former Leader of the Free World and his charmless former First Lady.

"Bill Clinton is very sexy," he insists.

"You think so?" I smile, being blind to the appeal of our nation's Seducer-in-Chief.

"Yes. Like you."

Meaning, I suppose, we're both husky old boys gone slightly to seed.

"Talk to me some more with your Bill Clinton voice."

Obviously, he doesn't hear the difference in intonation between an Arkansas and a North Carolina accent. To a Czech boy, a drawl is a drawl.

"Where are you from?" I ask.

"Brno. In the South. My family come to Prague after Havel for me to study music."

"What's your name?"

"Antonin. Please call me Tony."

"Antonin. Like Dvorak."

He sits up and stares as if he's astonished an American provincial is familiar with a national icon.

"Yes, of course," he says. "You like his music?"

"I don't know it that well," I admit.

"What is your work?" he asks.

How do I explain the mundane responsibilities of a Department of State civil servant with a Juris Doctor and a current assignment to the delegation in Brussels? I simply say I'm a lawyer.

"You like music?"

"Sure."

"You would like to hear me play?" The cubicle door is unlocked and a bald man with an enormous, lumpy head enters and starts stroking Tony's leg. The two Slavs have a brief exchange and the intruder leaves, closing the door.

"I tell him we are resting. He will be back," Tony giggles.

"I should go," I say. "It's a long ride back to my hotel."

"Where are you staying?

He whistles approvingly when I tell him the name of my hotel. Apparently, it's a destination for celebrities visiting Prague. Tony says Cher has stayed there. I mention a minor American television star drinking in the hotel bar last night, but the name means nothing to him. I ask if he'd like to stop by for a drink before I leave town.

"Oh, yes, of course. Tonight. Then we make love again. I will drive us."

His car isn't much of an improvement over the night tram. The heater's broken and the ashtray hasn't been emptied since the fall of the Communist regime. He doesn't seem to have mastered the art of braking, accelerating instead of slowing down as he navigates the hairpin turns on the narrow streets leading to the Castle District. I try to persuade myself that vehicular tragedy is impossible while the radio is broadcasting the serene *String Quartets Dedicated to Haydn.* But when he reaches for his ringing cell phone, I'm resigned to an obituary announcing I expired in a one-car collision while traveling in the Czech Republic. But Tony appears dexterous enough to drive and carry on a breakneck-speed conversation while lighting his cigarette. I recognize isolated words—he's speaking Russian now—and I know I'm the topic of discussion when he glances in my direction and giggles.

"My friend Yuri thinks you are very sexy."

"Does he like Bill Clinton, too?" I ask, bracing as we veer toward a delivery truck racing at us. Tony jerks the steering wheel with his palm and curses at the driver, who's blaring his horn, either a warning or a threat.

"Yuri would like to meet you."

The boys of Prague, butterflies they call them, have a reputation worldwide for seducing middle-aged tourists, lavishing them with attention until they're too enchanted to foresee that the none-too-happy ending of their little fairy tale is going to involve a black eye, broken nose and stolen wallet. The angel in the cubicle with the alabaster skin and innocent eyes is sprouting horns and a tail as he speaks.

"Well," I mumble, staying calm and collected, trying to allay any suspicion I'm on to him until I'm safely out of the car. When I hesitate, he says he doesn't want to share me with Yuri. He ends the call abruptly, then tosses the phone aside.

"What did you say to him?" I ask.

"I tell him to find his own American."

There's an awkward moment as we arrive at the Savoy. The doorman, a towering, regal Nigerian, seems a bit confused. He's not accustomed to the guests of this exclusive property arriving in rusty, dented deathtraps. Tony sits quietly, waiting for me to signal whether I'm going to invite or dismiss him. Knowing he's willing to surrender his car key—and the means for a quick, unobserved escape—makes me comfortable with my decision.

"Can you valet the car?" I ask the doorman.

"Of course, sir."

Tony's eyes widen as we step into the cozy lobby. He's craning his neck, hoping to find Cher or Miss Tina Turner holding court in the bar. What the hell, I decide, he looks more presentable in his tapered black pants and overcoat, a white silk scarf draped around his throat, than I do in my Carolina sports gear. He certainly won't be conspicuous among the guests having a quiet nightcap before retiring to their beds.

"Shall we have that drink?" I ask.

"Oh, yes," he says, his eyes dropping to his polished shoes. "But I have no money."

I tell him not to worry. If he's disappointed by the clientele, he doesn't show it. He doesn't recognize Madeline Albright, ensconced in a comfortable easy chair and sipping a cup of tea as she nods intently at the bullet-headed commissar who is quietly, but emphatically, making his point.

"Beer, wine or a cocktail?" I ask.

"Oh, prosecco! Please!"

The waiter, fey and obviously gay, smiles and says, "Of

course." I don't know if he's more amused by my young companion or by the idea I'm ordering a classic summer wine. Tony attacks the salty nibbles; I ask if he's eaten. Yes, yes, of course, he says, but he orders a cheeseburger and fries anyway.

"This is so nice, President Clinton," he laughs, oblivious to my distress that Madame Albright might have overheard his endearment. He's dragging the last fry through a dollop of ketchup when his phone rings.

"It is Yuri," he says, looking at the number flashing on the screen.

"Go ahead. Answer," I say.

I pour myself another glass of prosecco as they chat.

"He is very close," Tony says, holding the phone away from his face while he waits for my answer. "Just down the street."

Is the sweet, fizzy wine making me light-headed and obliterating my inhibitions and better judgment?

"Would he like to have a drink?"

Tony smiles and quickly closes the deal. I've got an immediate attack of buyer's remorse. What's going on with me? I'm about to make an even bigger ass of myself in full view of the former secretary of state.

"Now I am refreshed," he announces, emptying his glass. "Shall we have a bottle of red wine to warm us?"

Why not? At least Madame Albright won't be a witness. She and her companion are saying their good nights: thank you God for small kindnesses. This Yuri is likely to be a suspicious character, massive and austere, with a shaved head and scars, on holiday from his job as an enforcer for the Moscow mob— nothing at all like the cheery, cuddly teddy bear, no older than twenty-five, who wanders into the bar wearing a crinkly, crackling warm-up suit.

"Ah, Yuri, here we are," Tony calls out.

They kiss cheeks, right, then left, and Yuri flops beside me. He pulls off his wooly cap and plunges his stubby fingers into a mop of thick blond curls. He's a cherub to Tony's seraphim, with a toothy grin, plump cheeks and a stubborn case of hat-hair.

"You are a mess," Tony laughs. "Have a drink," he says, pouring glasses of burgundy and passing a lit cigarette to his friend. They speak as if they are alone, assuming, correctly, I'm not fluent in the language. The mumbled Russian words begin to sound ominous. The bartender stands sentinel, polishing the stemware with a clean white towel. Is the heavy red wine making me paranoid, or does he arch an eyebrow when I catch his eye? Is it a warning? A signal he's waiting for a sign to help me make my escape?

"Yuri thinks you are very sexy," Tony informs me, summoning the waiter and ordering another bottle of wine. Yuri confirms by reaching under the table and laying his hand on my crotch.

"Does Yuri speak English?"

"A little," Yuri answers. "I study in school."

He takes my hand and places it between his thighs, leaving no question about the healthy size of the swollen bulge in his shell suit.

"I think it would be very nice to kiss you," he whispers in halting English, nudging my foot with his bright red Adidas. I chuckle, then laugh out loud; Yuri seems puzzled by my unexpected reaction.

"Nothing, it's nothing," I say, certain he's never heard the old Elvis Costello song about angels and red shoes.

The three of us talk quietly, about pop stars and American movies. "Well, shall we?" Tony asks after we finish a third bottle of burgundy. He says Yuri must be up early in the morning. I don't remember extending an invitation for an overnight visit. As a matter of fact, I've never agreed that we will be going upstairs. So why am I following them to the lobby, acquiescent in whatever fate awaits me? The bartender's voice spins me on my heels.

"Sir, your room number please?"

I'm ready to plead guilty to as yet uncommitted crimes. Is he going to announce house rules—no unregistered guests in the room? Is he about to place a discreet call to hotel security and send them knocking on my door when my pants are around my ankles and my hands are otherwise engaged? But he simply hands me the bill for the food and wine, seeking my signature.

"Sorry," I apologize. "Sorry."

"No, sir, that is too generous," he says when he sees the gratuity I've added to the bill, a bribe for his discretion. I'm drunker than I ought to be. I insist he keep it.

"Please, sir, be careful," he says, touching my hand lightly. The chain mail band tattooed around his wrist is ominous.

"I'm fine," I say, ungratefully shrugging off his concern. This attack of paranoia is ridiculous, I decide. They're kids after all, boys from a provincial city, and I'm acting like a foolish American tourist, intimidated by their Iron Curtain accents and imperfect teeth.

Yuri is handing Tony a small, folded foil packet that he slips in his pocket as I approach.

"Ah, here you are at last!" he chirps, sweet and innocent as the bad seed. "It is time for fun!"

Yuri rubs against me in the tiny elevator, trying to mount me standing up. He reeks of tobacco and alcohol; fending off his passion, I wonder when his mouth last saw a toothbrush. I fumble with the key card, and Tony takes it from my hand and slips it into the slot. We stumble into the room, where Yuri strips so quickly I never see him undressing. He's on his knees, his face buried in my crotch. Tony is preoccupied with the image in the mirror, admiring himself, cocking his chin, assessing his profile, flinging his scarf from shoulder to shoulder.

"Do you think this is the room of Cher?" he asks. My tongue feels too thick to educate him about the pride of celebrities who would never sleep in anything smaller than a suite. "I think it is," he declares. "I would like very much to be fucked in the bed of Cher."

Yuri's body language doesn't indicate any interest in being fucked. He wrestles me to the bed. His soft baby fat is deceptively powerful, his strength the legacy of his peasant ancestors. He shoves his hand inside my shirt and pulls the hair on my chest. I'm distracted by the musk in his armpits and his dirty feet, but his prodigiously ample pink cock more than compensates for any deficiencies in hygiene.

"Come, Yuri," Tony beckons and they disappear behind the locked door of the bathroom. I sit on the edge of the bed, hesitant to remove so much as a shoe, and I take the opportunity to shove my wallet deep between the mattress and box spring. Knowing my passport and credit cards are locked in the safe doesn't relax me. I know I've made a huge mistake when I hear a glass shatter on the tile floor. The bathroom door opens and they trip into the bedroom laughing, their long cocks banging against their thighs. They're coke-jacked, edgy and impatient. Tony frowns, disappointed.

"You are still dressed?"

They stand on either side of me. Four hands unbuckle, unzip, untie my shoes and roll off my socks, strip off my jeans one leg at a time. Yuri laughs when he sees my baggy boxer shirts.

"American!" he announces, amused, his green eyes glassy, the left one slightly crossed.

I want to hand them a thousand *koruna* and call it a night, but it's too late to stop this runaway train without risking an angry confrontation. Tony drops to his knees and puts my cock in his mouth; the Russian runs his fingers through his friend's black hair, whispering Slavic endearments in his sweetest voice. Then he pushes Tony away and takes his turn biting and nibbling my shaft as Tony takes my face in both hands and kisses me.

"You sexy, sexy man," he purrs.

He crawls on the mattress and, steady on his hands and knees, tells me to spread his asscheeks. The tiny warts on his shaven pucker are oddly arousing; a faint whiff of the latex and lubricant lingers from the bathhouse.

"Now you will fuck me a long time," he says, slurring his words.

Only after I'm deep inside him do I realize I'm not wearing a condom, worry abandoned as I yield to Yuri's stubby fingers, first one, then two, probing my ass, loosening me enough to let him shove his enormous cock into my rectum without protest or resistance. It's been ages, years actually, since anyone has penetrated me, and Yuri is rough and insistent. He pushes Tony aside and flips me on my back. He orders Tony to pin my wrists to the mattress and grabs my ankles, hoisting my feet onto his shoulders. He's grunting like a wild beast, sweat pouring off his red face as he grinds his pelvis against the flesh of my buttocks, frustrated by his waning erection, the consequence of a nose full of coke. I know better than to agitate him any further and don't struggle while he tries stuffing his thick but limp penis into my ass. Tony strokes my face and, just before he plunges his tongue into my throat, his sweet voice assures me that I am, indeed, a sexy, sexy man. My cock grows hard as it's ever been and, not needing a hand or a mouth to bring me to the edge, I shoot farther than a man my age has any right to expect, splattering my semen over both of our faces.

* * *

I'm yanked from a dead stupor by a firm grip on my ankle, shaking my leg.

"Wake up, Mister Sleepyhead."

A simple hangover can't begin to describe the aftershocks rippling through my tannin-soaked brain. My muscles resist my feeble effort to haul myself off the mattress and confront the bright sunshine pouring through the window.

"You snore very much, all night," Tony laughs. He's standing over me fully dressed, his overcoat buttoned and his scarf knotted at his throat.

"Where is Yuri?" I ask as the dim memory of last night emerges from the thick fog of alcohol. I panic, imagining stolen cash and cards, then remember my wallet is safely tucked beneath the mattress.

"Oh, Yuri is gone to work many hours ago. He is a breakfast server at the Intercontinental. Not as nice as the Savoy," he sneers.

I pull a sheet around my waist and sigh, unable to find the energy to continue the conversation.

"Yuri is very upset I stay all night. He is very jealous."

Jealousy must have a very different meaning in Czech.

"Is he your boyfriend?"

"Not now," he says. "But he thinks so. It is time for me to go. You will be there at six tonight, of course. I am very excited you will hear me play."

He tells me not to lose the scrap of paper on which he's scribbled the location of this evening's concert. I say I'll try to make it, no promises. He laughs at my bravado, knowing the power of his smile over me.

"Do not be late. I will be looking for you when I walk onstage," he insists, turning to ask one last question before closing the door behind him.

"What is your name?"

"Bill," I admit.

"See you tonight, President Clinton."

The crowd gathering in the vast lobby of the Rudolfinum is dowdy, but prosperous. The women's shoulders are draped with bright Hermes scarves, adding a dash of color to their drab cloth coats. The husbands feign interest in their wives' idle chatter while checking their Rolexes every few seconds, impatient for the concert to begin. The doors to the recital hall open, and a plump matron in squeaky boots leads me to my seat. The room is overheated and I regret not checking my jacket.

I hadn't intended to be here. A repeat performance of last night's reckless and stupid behavior was out of the question. I'd crawled back into bed, mocked by the strip of unused condoms on the nightstand, dozing fitfully until the late afternoon, trying to forget my regrettable lack of judgment. When I finally staggered into the bathroom, I didn't recognize the stranger in the mirror. I splashed cold water on the raw skin where Tony had scratched my cheek. My boyish friends had pawed me like a pair of cats toying with a mouse before moving in for the kill, drawing blood, branding me with purple sucker bites on my throat and a grid of fiery welts covering my back. I scoured my body for bruises and nicks, aroused by the casual, impulsive damage they'd wreaked. My sudden, stubborn erection refused to fully recede even after I pumped a load of semen into the sink, banishing any possibility of a quiet evening of CNN and room service. I showered and dressed quickly, anxious to meet up again, already plotting tonight's encore as I rummaged in my bag for the digital camera to record our performance for posterity. The images would make quite an impression when that bastard in DC opened the attachments to my greetings from

Prague. At five forty-five, I was standing at the box office, ticket in hand.

He bursts on stage, leading a troupe of string players dressed in dark trousers and black silk shirts. He scans the front rows and, finding me, grins. He bows to the audience, a quick snap at the waist, then turns to face the ensemble, giving them a note to tune by. The program is little more than a classical jukebox selection of familiar movements from old warhorses: A bit of Vivaldi. Dvorak, of course: the *Prague Waltz*, a theme from *Humoresque*. I recognize the melody of Brahms's *Hungarian Dance*.

But his joy is infectious. The ensemble is clearly happy to defer to the virtuosity of a musical dervish, their first violinist. The audience demands an encore before departing for their dinners. Tony leads his players back onstage for a robust nightcap of Mozart, *Eine kleine Nachtmusik*, the perfect selection to bid us farewell.

A light snow is falling as the audience disperses into the night. The women cling to the arms of their companions as they negotiate the icy sidewalk. I stand by the doors, warming my hands in the pockets of my jacket, feeling conspicuous and foolish. The invitation was to hear him play, with no promise of a rendezvous, no designated meeting place. Ten, fifteen minutes pass and I finally accept that I'm waiting for someone who's probably halfway to his next destination—a café, a bar, the sauna. Yuri and he are off pursuing other prey tonight, fresh kill, leaving me standing on the steps to the concert hall, rejected and wallowing in self-pity, too self-absorbed to see Tony running toward me, his open overcoat flapping in the wind and white scarf dancing around his neck. He throws his arms around my neck and kisses my cheeks. The dark street seems less sinister now, the frigid wind less biting. The golems and nosferatus of this medieval city are in retreat, for the moment anyway. I point toward the castle on the hill, awash in brilliant electric light and tell Tony that his city is very beautiful.

"Prague is such a bore," he says dismissively. "So small and dull. There is no opportunity for a musician here."

He hails a cab and we squeeze into the tight backseat, balancing his violin case on our knees.

"We must hurry," he says. "We are very late."

He speaks to the driver, giving the address of our destination, I assume. I don't ask where Yuri awaits us. My erection is straining against the fabric of my pants, aroused by the many possibilities. The sauna again? A deluxe cabin big enough for three and any curious stranger they invite to share me? A sex club with a corridor of glory holes and a leather sling? Maybe something more romantic? A dance club and a couple of bottles of cheap champagne, a prelude to another powder-fueled liaison at the Savoy?

"Ah, here we are," he says as the driver stops in front of a nondescript building on a quiet side street. He sits clutching his violin case until I understand I'm expected to pay the fare. A gentleman in black tie greets us at the door and takes our coats and the violin case. The dining room is small, a dozen tables with crisp white tablecloths and bud vases with a single carnation and a sprig of asparagus fern. The waiter is carrying plates of homey fare, aromatic roast pork and beef, simmered for hours in broth laced with garlic and paprika. It appears Tony has decided on a romantic evening. I scan the room, looking for a thick mop of blond curls among the gray and balding heads. I'm a little puzzled about the rush, since it appears Yuri has yet to arrive. The maitre d' leads us to a table in a far a corner and motions for us to sit. It's obviously a mistake. A woman, matronly but not yet old, is already seated, still dressed for the outdoors in a fur hat and unbuttoned overcoat. Tony bends to kiss her cheeks and helps her with her coat. He speaks quietly, in a deferential voice; I understand my name and that I am being introduced. The woman smiles at me, dignified but friendly.

"I am pleased for you to meet my mother," he says proudly.

He orders a sherry for his mother and two tall glasses of pilsner for him and me. They chatter in Czech. I know I am the topic of conversation; his mother is inspecting me, nodding approvingly. Yuri obviously is not expected to join us as there are only place settings for three.

"I shall order for the table, okay?" he announces. "You must know my favorite foods."

He seems to point to every item on the menu as the waiter scribbles furiously on his notepad. We have a while to relax before the meal is served. Tony and his mother share the same blue eyes and dimpled chin. I see what he will look like in a decade or two when the Czech diet has softened his sharp features. He clasps my left hand and his mother's right, as solemn as a minister about to unite until death do us part.

"Mama thinks you are very handsome and would have beautiful children," he says.

Mama must be very naïve, assuming I'm a paterfamilias who's taken an inexplicable interest in her son.

"Mama says I am very lucky to marry an American," he laughs, scratching my palm with his index finger. "She says we must have a big apartment and she will visit us at Easter and the Christmas holiday. What do you think?" he asks, dazzling me with his ingratiating smile.

Preposterous, impossible, ridiculous, out of the question, I silently protest as I squeeze his hand. His charms and prodigious appetites aren't powerful enough to bewitch the jaded cynic I've become. But my flight doesn't depart for three more days.

There's no reason to disappoint him, not just yet. He slips off his shoe and, burrowing his foot under the cuff of my pants, tickles my calf with his toes. I blush, mortified by the blood shamelessly rushing to my penis, undeterred by the matriarch smiling at me across the table. He arches his eyebrow, gently mocking me, his willing captive, knowing there's time enough to keep stirring his cauldron until, steeped in his intoxicating brew of sex, charm, beauty and affection, refusing him will be impossible and I will happily embrace my fate.

THAT EMBRACE

Andy Quan

The crowd outside the chapel was bigger than the one inside; the family had perhaps not understood Adrian's reach and effect. I stood just outside the doorway. If I strained, I could see the face of the person speaking at the pulpit, but I felt I didn't deserve a nearer place or better view.

What I learned but hadn't known: he had two brothers and two sisters; he made up nicknames for friends and acquaintances; he was a doting uncle; he was a joker from a young age. It wasn't explained, but I learned from others before and afterward that he'd been raised in a strongly conservative suburb, a village unto itself so cut off was it from other neighborhoods. That perhaps explained the silence on his sexuality, even obfuscation, as a group of childhood friends eulogized about *what a ladies' man he was.*

From the website of the judo club that he'd helped start, I learned of his kindness and the mutual devotion between teacher and students. Particularly touching was one testimonial from a mother of five. *Adrian encouraged me to be someone I never believed I could be.* So, it was natural the crowd was filled with fellow martial artists and students, including an old Korean master, who brought tears to all when he conveyed upon his old student, posthumously, the next level of his discipline's mastery.

I hadn't known Adrian's age. From the strong features of his face and his athlete's body, I'd assumed he was older than me, not six months younger. I wasn't aware of his passion for U2. His sister described his dissection of their latest album and his joyful, shirtless dancing at their last concert. They'd chosen the group's quietest and most mournful songs to precede and end the ceremony.

Most of the speakers referred to his charisma, how handsome he was, his startling blue eyes, the bulging muscles of his arms and torso.

This I knew.

After a few false starts, I'd settled into a comfortable apartment and neighborhood in Sydney ten years ago and joined the local gym. The atmosphere was friendly enough, though I hadn't broken the ice with many other gym-goers. The trick, it seemed, was to start the conversation outside of the gym. That's how I met Les and Simon, at a gay bar on a hot summer day. Simon was the talker, an extrovert, who looked familiar enough, though I'd definitely seen his partner, who looked like Mr. Clean, tall with a shaved head and broad shoulders. It turned out that they were the eyes and ears of the gym, combining forces to make friends and gossip about the rest.

They knew who was gay (most of the gym), who had been going out with who, how long they'd been members. Casually, I'd asked them about Adrian. Not that I knew his name. I'd just been entranced by his attractiveness and the bright smile that shone out of his square jaw.

"Yeah, he is handsome," commented Simon. "Went out with a girl who worked at the front desk for a while, but people talk. We're not sure about him." Sexuality was what he was referring to.

"Have you seen his head, though?" quizzed Les. He was the cattier of the two, though somehow managed to sound factual rather than mean. "He keeps his head shaved, but you can still see where the hair plugs went in."

This needed some explaining to me. I'd only vaguely heard about hair transplantation techniques, a vanity I was unfamiliar with, though in the setting of our gym, or our gay lives, it didn't seem too unusual. We all worked out feverishly before dance parties so we could take our shirts off and be either proud of the results or at least unembarrassed. Steroids weren't uncommon: how else could there be so many perfect muscle gods in Sydney? A few friends had surprised me by confessing to Botox treatments. "Well, of course *you* wouldn't need it! You're Asian. But look at the wrinkles on this white face!" Glen told me. "It's the sun. We age pretty quickly here." Someone had even pointed out a pec implant to me at a dance party. "Look at it. It's a beautiful shape." We were checking out the ample chest of one man. "But it doesn't really move when his arms do." I admitted that he was right.

"Are you looking sad, disgusted or judgmental?" asked Les.

It was the first. Such effort for something that had clearly not worked out.

It was the start of a new century and my early days of dance parties in Sydney, of gathering with huge numbers of gay men and their friends to dance in various states of undress the whole night through, on a variety of mood-altering substances, though ecstasy was most prevalent, the pills with the happy-face that had really started the phenomenon. Yes, queens had been getting high and naked since the seventies, but the end of the eighties had brought a worldwide phenomenon that had crossed into the mainstream, no longer limited to sexual deviants.

Though in Sydney, we still ruled the place. There were the famous Mardi Gras and Sleaze parties, but as well a New Year's party and the leather-clad Inquisition event. Sydney groovers knew they were the best parties. I was still relatively innocent in my drug taking, and hadn't moved on to other letters. E was enough and with luck, it brought the energy to stay awake, a euphoric horniness and a feeling of great love for anyone in sight.

I was by myself at Hand in Hand, a medium-sized party held as a fundraiser for the state HIV organization, dancing in the middle of a sea of people, when I saw a familiar face a number of feet away. He caught my eye, and decisively made his way over to me.

"I'm Adrian."

I introduced myself. "I've seen you at the gym but never had the chance to say hello."

"And how's your party?" And at that moment, he wrapped his arms around me in a warm embrace. I placed my arms around his back. That's how it began. I'd like to report a romantic encounter, but it's not discretion holding me back. It didn't happen. Instead, never letting me go, we talked, or simply held each other, for hours. I don't even know what we talked about. But I felt happy and safe.

His body really was one of the most remarkable I'd had contact with. All of his muscles were in perfect definition, a latticework around his stomach and up around his back, his strong chest, his biceps and forearms. Gay men in Sydney work out constantly at gyms, but fewer are athletes; his body was built through activity and sport rather than weights alone.

Whatever combination of our moods, I wasn't feeling particularly sexual. I let my hands roam over his strong body but with more curiosity than intent. I would occasionally lift my head up toward his, angling for a kiss, for something more, but Adrian kept holding me, jovial and warm, like a friend, seemingly unaware of how beautiful I considered him.

When I told this story recently to a friend, he asked sharply, "Weren't you embarrassed, both of you? What did other people think of you locked together like that?"

What I remember: one of his friends, Japanese Kaz with the dyed blond hair, dancing with us for a while; and being surprised at the end of the evening that we'd held each other the whole night through. I remembered little else and not a shred of shame.

Les and Simon made fun of me for years afterward. Mainly because I would look for Adrian every dance party for the next year or two, hoping to repeat the experience, but the few times I saw him I would only get a short hello; not unfriendly, mind you, but he was with friends, or on his way out, and the experience was not to be repeated.

There was a small possibility that if I'd been more assertive, if I'd known what I wanted, if I'd had the confidence to believe I could have gotten it, I might have had a less chaste encounter. But that was not who I was.

I continued to see Adrian at the gym. We never had long conversations but would ask after each other. He would ask whether I was going to the next dance party. Occasionally I'd find out how his martial arts competitions were going. I Googled him once and found the website of the club. I found a few photos of him, admired his looks, remembered our encounter and idly imagined signing up for his class.

Through the grapevine, I found out more about his personal life. The first time I'd seen Kaz after the party, I'd asked him whether Adrian was gay. "You'll have to ask him about that," he'd advised and smiled awkwardly. It came out that he was with a man, another fitness trainer, for about ten years. For part of that time, he was also with a woman for three years. It sounded confusing and not particularly happy.

He also went out to gay clubs and partied too hard. He was sometimes unreliable and missed showing up for his appointments with clients. "I've seen him when he looks like he's still off his face," said Les, critical again. "Or maybe he was just tired, but I wouldn't want to train with someone like that. You could hurt yourself."

I slowed down my partying, and even the events that I went to, I never spotted Adrian again at them. My friends did though— and a few reported his appearing in a crowd and locking them in a big slobbery kiss. They knew I was jealous but assured me that it wasn't a pleasant experience. One year at the gym, we talked about his upcoming trip to Mykonos and Ibiza. He was planning on partying at some of the biggest clubs in Europe on hot Mediterranean evenings. I imagined the men that he would meet and bed.

Over the years, I heard less about Adrian's martial arts competitions. I wasn't sure if he still taught. He also got bigger, year after year. I had imagined it impossible; in my mind, he was as muscular as could be, with perfect proportions. But Adrian obviously didn't feel that way. His muscles grew. They became more angular. He looked more like a bodybuilder than a martial artist. But rather than looking more healthy, he appeared tired with lines under his eyes.

Only a year ago, something strange was happening to him. Les and Simon had joined a new gym and left ours, but a new friend, Ger, was not only full of gossip, but had started training with Adrian.

"Why does Adrian look so dark?" I'd asked. "His skin has gone a different color, but it doesn't look like a tan."

"I know. Isn't it awful? It's experimental. Some sort of injection, he's on some trial of it."

But the effect was disconcerting: his skin tone didn't match his Anglo-Saxon features. He was darker on the upper part of his body, while his legs were lighter. I couldn't help but take part in a running commentary with Ger over the weeks about how awful it looked. It was also clear that Adrian's increase in size and muscularity was through steroids. The veins on his arms stood out. Occasionally, when I saw him, I still imagined feeling his amazing body, but it was also off-putting. It had become harder, more boxy and less welcoming. I noticed, once, when he was saying hello, that his voice was scratchy and low, a cold I'd assumed, and then after time, he couldn't seem to get rid of it because he was doing too much partying.

The last times I saw Adrian, he had reverted to a more natural color. His body was still imposing, But he seemed run down. In the meantime, I was turning forty and thinking about aging. I'd settled into a happy three-year relationship, barely went out and hadn't partied in ages. Because it was so different from my drug-fueled discovery of Sydney as a single man, it had caused introspection. I came to admit to myself that I'd turned some of those substance-enhanced encounters and friendships into myth and romance, and romanticized bonds that had only been possible because both parties were high.

The very last time I saw Adrian, I'd thought about this. I certainly wouldn't erase our embrace from my memory but felt some embarrassment for my young, naïve self, searching him out at dance parties, and the way that instead of accepting and valuing experiences, I tried to recreate them and seek out more.

We left the gym at the same time, and I noticed, with some shock, that his voice was still gravelly after what I remembered as months since it first started. On the street as we parted, I put my hand on his back. I felt a shiver of attraction from the heat of his body. "You've got to take better care of yourself," I told him. He replied in a tone both jovial and self-conscious that he was trying.

Two mornings later, when he failed to show up for a training session, his client, who was also a friend and pissed-off, went to Adrian's apartment to give him a lecture on unreliability. But seeing that Adrian was apparently home—his car parked out front—but did not answer the door, he got worried and called the police. It was too late to revive Adrian. He'd died.

None of us knew the family well enough to inquire about what happened, and we weren't even sure if a comprehensive toxicology was done before his body was cremated less than a week later. But I found out that he'd had a tumor removed from his throat, which was the real excuse for his change of voice. I found from the Internet that the possible side-effects of inject-able tanning treatments are unproven, and doctors worry that tricking the body into believing it is exposed to the sun might cause cancer. I learned that Adrian had been hospitalized before and told to stop the treatment but that he'd continued. I worried that he'd been out partying at a club and taken a substance like GHB from which acquaintances had died in the past. But no, he'd been teaching a judo class the night before. So, I wondered if his kidney or liver had shut down from steroids and the tanning hormones and maybe even something he was taking for the cancer.

Death by tanning is one of the stupidest ways I've ever heard of to die. I heard of a beautiful man, also gay, also muscular, who had gone in for a nose job and died of a staph infection, and dying from plastic surgery also rates highly. But the facts of his death dishonor Adrian, make him sound monstrous; what I'd heard at the funeral told me that he was caring and loving, and cared and loved, and that he took care of others even though he didn't take care of himself.

I wonder how being attracted to men played into this story. He certainly struggled with it. He came from a background that if not homophobic, was not supportive. The archetypal story of a gay man not accepting his sexuality mirrors a man who does not accept his own body or skin.

I mourned Adrian and I imagined talking to him. *Did anyone ever tell you how beautiful you were? That you had no need for a different skin color and more muscles? Was it self-hatred or careless experimentation? I am angry that you wasted a life.*

Another lesson of getting older is how people come and go. Settling into a relationship and a routine, settling out of going to bars and parties, I realize there are acquaintances who I haven't seen for years, some who moved abroad and I'd find out after the fact. At the gym, Adrian's memorial photo disappeared surprisingly quickly and the place and its members put back on their workout clothes and gloves, leather filled with sweat and grains of salt.

It seems cliché to say that it seemed like he'd simply gone on another trip to Ibiza or started personal training at another gym. Cruel, too, when others closer to him would still bear their different weight of grief. But it's easier to think that way. I had such a tiny window into his kind, troubled soul, to a more truthful self beyond his dazzling appearance.

Adrian Miles, I'll fold this glimpse of you into my hands, tuck into it that one embrace and hide it away.

Good-bye.

ON SPANKING THE MOST BEAUTIFUL BOY IN THE WORLD

Simon Sheppard

He was, yes, the most beautiful boy in the world, assuming that someone liked lithe young blonds with adorable faces. And at least one particular someone, a middle-aged man named Chris, certainly did. Chris adored them, couldn't help staring at them when they passed him on the street, masturbated to images of them when he was at home alone in front of his computer.

He'd ended up in the cluttered bedroom of the boy—who was also named Kris, but Kris with a K, not a C-H—by sort of a lucky accident. The exact circumstances, though on the amusing side, weren't really important. What was important was that he was in the very same room as the most beautiful boy in the world, the entire world. What was improbable was that the boy wanted to have sex with him, in fact already had what seemed, again for all the world, to be a hard-on in his sweatpants. What was absolutely wonderful is that the boy, Kris, had told him that he liked to be spanked.

It was all so easy, so perfect, that Chris thought Kris might have been figuring that an exchange of money would be involved. This would not have been horrible. It might even have answered the question of why young, blond Kris had invited over the older man, with his male pattern baldness, slight paunch, and presentable-but-weathered face, when the boy could, presumably, have had just about anyone he chose. But when Chris had gingerly broached the subject, afraid that Kris might be offended but even more afraid of some awkward misunderstanding farther down the line, he was reassured when Kris simply smiled and said that cash was the last thing on his mind.

Then he leaned over and kissed the older man softly on the cheek, a gesture that, unexpectedly, almost brought Chris to tears. *Better get ahold of myself,* he thought. *I don't want to look like some helpless, foolish old man.*

Kris seemed not to notice, however. He stood and peeled off his shirt, taking care to keep his baseball cap on. Chris stifled a gasp. The boy's torso was the cliché of a stereotype of an ideal—smooth, just lightly defined, with small, but not too small, pink nipples.

"So what do you want to do?" Kris asked.

Everything, Chris thought.

Everything.

Waiting for an answer, Kris smiled uncertainly. For the first time, Chris saw his young companion as something less than his seemingly unattainable dream made flesh, achingly accessible flesh. He was just a young man, somewhat unsure of himself, with a symmetrical face crowned by a shock of cornflower-colored hair, a lucky accident of genetics. Chris wondered what it would be like to be him. Was he aware of how much an object of desire he was, how he possessed the power to break old men's hearts, or at least *one* old man's heart? It was, Chris knew, a question he would never, should never, ask. The boy would, like all things of great beauty, remain a mystery.

Chris, with just a bit of hesitation, began to unbutton his own shirt.

"No," Kris said. "I'd prefer if you kept your clothes on."

Chris couldn't decide whether he should take that as a relief or a mild rebuke. But as soon as Kris began pulling off his sweatpants, it seemed irrelevant. The boy wasn't wearing under-wear—something of a disappointment to Chris, who preferred his spankings to start with a boy wearing jockey shorts before progressing to bare bottom. Still, Kris apparently knew what he was doing. He edged the waistband of his red sweatpants partway down—low enough to reveal the top curve of a smooth ass, a heartbreakingly lean belly hairless all the way down to a fringe of pubic hair—then stopped.

If there were a mirror around, Chris was convinced, he would see on his face the look of a starving man.

"So, you going to spank me or what?"

Too abrupt. But what was Chris, jolted from his reverie, going to say? *No?*

"Sure. You like it over the knee?"

"If you do." This was not the way the most beautiful boy in the world was supposed to behave. Too curt, too matter-of-fact. This was the way a somewhat impatient, horny twenty-year-old would act. The way, face it, Kris was acting. He wanted the boy to have a soul as beautiful as his body. But it was what it was; he'd make do.

"Sure." Chris rearranged himself on the bed so Kris could lie on his lap. Fortunately, the boy didn't pull his pants any farther down. His hard crotch was pressed up against Chris's lap, his pale ass half-exposed and waiting.

Chris raised his right hand, wishing he weren't feeling that the next few minutes would probably be the crowning moment of his life. But there it was. The crowning moment of his life. His hand trembled slightly.

"Go on, spank me," the amazing young man whispered, slightly impatient.

Chris's hand came down. The blow struck the thick cloth of the sweatpants, resulting in a muffled *whap*. Kris said nothing, didn't moan. He pushed his butt up for more.

Another slap, then another. Chris would have liked to expose the beautiful boy's entire ass, but he hesitated, afraid the perfect moment would come and then be gone.

A few blows later, the boy beat him to it. Kris reached back and pulled down the seat of his pants.

His ass was every bit as gorgeous as Chris had expected, had hoped. More so. The flesh was flawlessly formed, pale, smooth. There was just one small blemish, like the flaw a Persian rug-maker purposely leaves in his carpet to acknowledge that only Allah can make a perfect thing. But blasphemy or no, the boy was perfect: fantastic, unforgettable.

Chris stroked the boy's butt, his palm gliding over young skin. He gently parted the cheeks, exposing the crack hairy with blond fur, the hole pink and relaxed, gateway to some eternal secret.

Chris shook his head. *Listen to myself. What a pretentious load of bullshit.* But, thoroughly besotted by the half-naked boy slung over his lap, he really had no choice but to forgive his own excesses. *As I forgive those who excess against me,* he thought, almost giggling inappropriately.

He bent over and inhaled deeply: just the slightest intoxicating hint of musk. Left to his own devices, he would have leaned down and kissed and tongued the dangerous wrinkle of flesh. But Kris had been quite clear, very definite: "You can spank me, from medium to pretty intense, but no sex, though you can milk my cock if you want." Chris was a man of honor, sure, but more than that, a creature of practicality. Now that he had his hands, quite literally, on Kris, he wasn't going to make some stupid move that might endanger the whole thing. With one final, deep inhalation, he straightened up. His dick was throbbing, hard.

"You can spank me some more if you want to." It sounded less like a suggestion than a command. Chris found himself wondering whether he wouldn't feel so powerless if he were paying. His hand came down on the boy's ass.

"You can go harder."

Chris knew when he was licked. Yes, he almost wished that money *had* changed hands.

Still, he was supposed to be the Daddy in all this. Time to assert himself. "Stand up and take those pants off," he said. "Then I'll spank your ass some more."

To Chris's delight and mild surprise, the boy stood up and gracelessly lowered his red sweatpants.

The boy's hard dick was unexpected. Though it was satisfyingly long and thick, it had a pronounced, almost freakish, downward curve.

Chris adored it.

He didn't ask for permission, but fished out his own swelling cock. Kris had stepped out of his sweatpants and stood waiting, naked except for half-length white gym socks and that stupid, iconic baseball cap.

"Get back on my lap."

"Yes, Daddy." It was the first time Kris had used the *D*-word, which they'd used when they'd set up the date, but had so far today only been hovering in the background like some chronological ghost.

Now that the naked boy was back across his legs, bare dick

against bare dick, Chris reached down and knocked the cap off his head. It tumbled to the floor. Chris grabbed a handful of the shock of honey-colored hair. Rather than objecting, Kris moaned softly. Chris pulled, bending the beautiful boy's head slightly back, as he brought his other hand down on the naked, pink ass. Kris spread his legs, his downward-curving cock showing hard between his smooth, nearly hairless thighs.

Chris couldn't resist. He swatted Kris's ass a few more times, ramping up a little, turning the flesh a darker pink, then moved his right hand down to the boy's dick, grabbing hold of the shaft. Kris moved his ass a little higher so the older man could get a better grip. Chris let go, spit into his hand, then reached down and starting "milking," as Kris had said, the boy's cock.

Heaven. It was absolute heaven to watch the naked young man squirm.

When he awoke, the half-finished story was still on the desktop of his Mac. Reading it over in the clear light of morning, it seemed more than a bit florid. How to make the theoretical reader understand, empathize? How to hint at the ineffable, the transcendent, without lapsing into pretentious twaddle? Ah, well, he'd have to work on that.

He checked his email.

When, the night before, he'd first started working on the story, he had, of course, thought back to the real-life boy who'd inspired him. The kid's name wasn't Kris though, it was Kyle, and the boy might not have been quite as perfect as the narrator, with his literary license, was making him out to be.

And musing on Kyle, he'd realized he really wanted to spank someone. Truth to tell, it had been months, and now just thinking about reddening a younger guy's butt had made his dick swell. He'd opened up Craigslist and posted an ad. *Dad wants to spank you,* the headline read, and it went on predictably from there.

The first response he'd gotten was, maybe surprisingly but probably not, from Kyle; since the ad had no pictures, the kid would have had no idea who'd placed it. *Spank me, Daddy,* the email's subject line had read.

Hi, Kyle, he'd emailed back. *It's me. I'd love to get together again.* And, for identification, he'd included a photo of his face.

But—not entirely to his surprise—there had been no response from Kyle. And although there had been a few more emails from other potential spankees, none of them panned out...pretty much par for the course for Craigslist. Fortunately, he was able to multitask, and he cruised online while he worked on the short story, and, eventually, jacked off. Finally he hit SAVE one more time and went to bed.

And now, the next morning, still nothing from Kyle, the putative "most beautiful boy in the world."

But the story, half-finished, sat there as a somewhat over-written reproach: *If you're going to obsess over spanking an impossible object of desire, dude, don't be surprised if you come up empty handed.*

He sighed and got back to work.

Chris tried to memorize every detail.

The sound of Kris's voice. Every inch of the boy's creamy flesh, every gleaming curve. Even the boy's smells; Chris ran a hand along Kris's armpit, then brought it to his nose and inhaled. Not bad: no deodorant, but another couple of days without a shower would have made things even more heady.

And then he wanted, simultaneously, two contradictory things.

He wanted to worship the boy, to prostrate himself before the impossible glory of the kid.

And he wanted to hurt him.

And yet, since Kris *wanted* to be hurt, wasn't spanking him in fact serving him? Wasn't his turning himself into a sadistic monster a sacrifice to Kris?

And then Kris said, with a definite undertone of impatience, "What's the problem?"

Chris looked down at the boy's big, perfectly formed feet. He longed to grovel at those feet, have them rubbed in his face, to live for nothing but those feet. And to beg for mercy.

Instead he slapped Kris's ass. Hard. Much harder than before. And then harder still.

Now it was obvious that the spanking was no longer just some game. Kris had turned down the offer of a safeword, and Chris had assured him that he knew how to read a bottomboy's body language, that limits would be honored. Now all of that was not anywhere near so clear.

Because if he couldn't possess such beauty, he would hurt it.

Kris was squirming for real now, crying out in pain. His ass was red, not pink, and burning hot to the touch, its surface mottled by a network of busted capillaries.

Was Kris sobbing?

"You...little...cunt," Chris gritted out.

And then he brought himself up short. What did he want out of this? And he wondered whether he was asking this about the boy or about himself. Or both. His hand hurt.

"*Now* what's the matter?" Kris complained.

"Fuck you!" Chris yelled and hit the perfect boy's ass again. Now Kris *was* sobbing, and Chris didn't care. He hit him until the boy tried to squirm away, to escape the pain. Chris held him down, though, and kept pummeling the boy's abused butt.

"Okay, enough," Kris said, firmly.

Chris snapped out of it and backed off, staring down at the

boy's bruised and battered ass. Everything was spinning. He wondered if he'd gone too far. He *had* gone too far.

And then Kris slid off the older man's lap and looked up at him, the boy's face flushed, his eyes brimming with tears. He smiled, his lips quivering, and then put his face to Chris's and gave him a gentle, lingering kiss. Just one. Then he stood shakily up, grabbed his own curved cock and frantically jacked himself off until he'd shot streams of cum all over the place.

Chris looked down. Almost without noticing, he'd shot off, too. His pants were a mess.

"What's funny?" the boy asked.

"Nothing." Chris hadn't even known he was smiling.

Chris took a while to get himself together. Kris, meanwhile, had wiped off but was still—to Chris's infinite gratitude—naked. His ass would, clearly, take a while to get back to normal. They made the usual awkward post-trick conversation until Chris was ready to go.

"Well, thanks," Chris said, heading for the door. He glanced down at the red sweatpants lying in the corner; he would have liked to bury his face in them, inhale the scent into his memory, but it would have been unseemly.

"So when will you be available again?" Kris asked.

"You want to do this some more?" Chris hoped his tone wasn't too hopeful; wasn't too desperate, too incredulous. Just matter-of-fact.

"Sure."

Chris knew that seeing the boy again was improbable—but possible, since stranger things had happened. Things like his having spanked the most beautiful boy in the world until they both came.

At the moment he walked out of the boy's apartment, Chris felt, no doubt foolishly, that he was walking out of Paradise.

He had, back in college, been something of a classical scholar, though he'd ended up in real estate, and he thought at that moment of the Emperor Hadrian. Hadrian's young boyfriend, the impossibly beautiful Antinous, had drowned in the Nile, and the emperor had subsequently made him a god, filling his domain with statues of his dead love. If Chris were a sculptor, he mused, he would immortalize Kris in marble. If he were an author, he would write books about his heartbreaking loveliness, scrupulously listing every detail. But Chris was a realtor, and the most he could imagine himself doing would be naming a street in a housing development "Kris Way." Pathetic.

And now, in any case, he was the one who was drowning.

Tears came again to his eyes and this time, in the dark, he allowed himself to cry.

He was just a fool. A silly old fool.

Just like lovesick Hadrian.

Oh, well.

THE INNER GAME OF CHESS

Cecilia Tan

Richard Partridge would like to state for the record that even though when he sits down at the chessboard he wants his opponent to think he's much older than he is, he is not actually that many years older than Topher Lin; five, to be exact.

When Richard was fourteen and winning high school chess tournaments and Topher was nine and already cleaning up at regional events, the five years seemed both an enormous gulf— Topher was just a *child!*—and nowhere near enough time to prepare for the little genius's arrival as an eventual challenger.

Topher's own father, the venerable and respected chess master John Lin, had joked at the time that Richard had better hurry up and go pro, or Topher was going to catch him.

Or maybe it wasn't a joke. Richard certainly hadn't taken his mentor's words that way. He had gone pro before he was out of high school.

Now, though, Topher is the one out of high school, a freshman at college somewhere. Richard sits across from him and flashbulbs pop as they reach over the board to shake hands. Topher is Richard's height now, his glossy black hair carelessly long, as if he's so busy playing chess that a mundane task like visiting the barber is beneath him. Or maybe his mother still cuts it with him sitting in a kitchen chair. Richard holds on to that image, of skinny-legged twelve-year-old Topher with a bowl over his head, fidgeting because he wants to get back to the study where Richard and Master Lin are having a chess lesson.

The image shreds before Topher's perfect smile and seductive beauty. Richard catches himself staring. His old mentor's son has grown up to be fashion-model pretty, half Chinese, half Czech. The sleeves of his suit are a little too short, but instead of looking like his mother bought the suit two years ago and Topher's been too oblivious to get rid of it, it looks somehow like that must be the fashion these days.

Richard focuses far too much on the boy across from him and way too little on the board between them. Topher demolishes him as the endgame nears. Flashbulbs blind Richard again as he lays down his king in resignation, thinking to himself that the kid isn't that cute after all. Which is a damn good thing, because Master Lin would surely have a stroke if he had any idea that his former student had any kind of improper thoughts about his young son. Ever.

Richard goes home to his rent-controlled East Village apartment and sulks for about five minutes. Then he dresses, walks to a dance club in Alphabet City he likes, and goes home with a guy who never asks his name, and that's just fine with him. Topher Lin is gone from his thoughts. *Poof.*

Two weeks later Richard is forcibly reminded of Topher when he reads the *Chess Monthly* piece about their match. It wasn't even that important a match, but the writer had blown it all out of proportion, how Richard had been mentored by Master Lin, how he'd slept on the Lins' couch and helped them rake leaves and mowed their lawn, like some modern-day kung fu training story, except with chess. They're obviously trying to make some kind of rivals out of them, him and Topher.

Rival schmival. Richard throws the magazine into the recycling bin before getting to the part of the article about how Topher is in his first year at Columbia University. Thus he is surprised when he is driving home one night from a house party up in Riverdale, winding his way through the Village to his building, and he sees Topher on a street corner.

It isn't just that he sees Topher on a street corner. He sees him kissing someone. And it isn't just that he's kissing someone. He's kissing a man. Or a boy. Richard doesn't stop to check the guy's ID. He does stop to grab Topher by the scruff of the neck like a naughty puppy and stuff him into the passenger seat of the car, peeling out seconds later with the scent of burned rubber reflecting how scorched he feels inside.

"What the hell do you think you're doing?" Richard demands, gunning through a yellow light and onto FDR Drive.

Topher, for his part, looks subdued, perhaps sullen, but not openly defiant, except for the fact that he doesn't answer.

"Just because you're at college now and away from your parents doesn't mean you can...can...go crazy," he rants. "You could get raped. You could get AIDS."

Richard expects Topher to argue. To shoot back with something like, *Who do you think you are, my father?*

But all Topher says, when Richard pauses for a breath, is "I'm sorry to have disappointed you," with his face turned toward the passenger-side window, as if the side of the road is fascinating to him.

Why? Richard thinks. *Why do you have to be so perfect, Topher Lin? It's like you popped out of the womb the prince of the chess world. You won't even deign to speak to mere peons like me.*

Now the only sound is the engine and the tires, as Richard takes out his frustrations on the road and the other drivers.

Topher breaks the silence. "I'm over eighteen, you know."

Richard makes a disgusted noise. "And that makes it okay to play tonsil hockey on the street? Where someone might see you?"

"Someone like who? It's not as if a photographer from *Chess Monthly* follows me around." Now Topher stretches in the bucket seat of the sports car, and Richard tries not to look at how long his limbs are, like a cat's, elongating as he stretches. "It's not like anyone's going to recognize me—"

"I recognized you!" Richard pulls off the street and screeches to a halt by a fire hydrant.

"But you know me!" Topher meets his stare, finally, and his eyes are wide and shiny like black jade buttons. "Is it an international incident that I do something other than play chess and study?"

"Get out of the car."

"What?"

"Get out!"

Topher throws up his hands and pushes open the door. He's barely slammed it before Richard is pulling away. It takes a few blocks for Richard to calm down enough to notice where he is. Upper East Side—safe enough for walking. He drives downtown, thinking about Topher Lin the entire ride.

Topher Lin, for his part, finds the entire thing a puzzle. This whole business about kissing people in general is highly confusing to begin with, which is half what he finds interesting about it. The urge to explore has been there for a while, but living at home and being constantly busy with chess while applying to colleges stifled exploration. Partridge is right, of course. Now that he's living away from home for the first time, he has a chance to experience some things he hasn't before, and he is approaching the world just as methodically as he would a new opponent.

He's just as busy now, of course, if not even more, trying to keep up with both chess and term papers. He definitely doesn't have time for a girlfriend, and this is one of the reasons kissing boys has become something of a strategy. A girl, Topher has learned, will want to spend two hours going bowling, or walking in the park and eating a meal, or seeing a movie together, before she'll kiss him. Whereas boys couldn't care less about appearances or whether you bought them dinner. Much simpler. Also, Topher is somewhat intimidated by the female anatomy and has resolved not to learn about it until he actually *needs* to.

He thinks he's pretty much figured out boys, though, at least the kind who will kiss him when he wants, and who will help him get off if he returns the favor—usually with mutual hand jobs in a restroom. He rides the train back to the campus now, staring at the window without really seeing the tunnel going by outside as he tries to work through the new puzzle that is Richard Partridge.

Topher's known him as far back as he can remember, it seems. And Richard was always the one Topher looked up to, the big brother he never had. The one with the cool handheld video game, the high-tech phone, the car—and yet all Richard ever really seemed to care about was chess. It's not so different now, Topher supposes. Richard has designer suits and an impeccably stylish haircut and a fancier, more expensive car...and why the hell does he care what Topher does, anyway?

Maybe Richard does think about something other than chess. Or is this not about chess at all?

Topher's thoughts suddenly tumble in another direction, as if he sees the board from a new angle. It's not about chess, except that it is about Richard and Topher. Now that he glimpses a new way to attack the problem, he wants to try it out right away. He wants to maneuver his queen into position and corner him and see how he reacts.

In the morning, he gets Richard's phone number and address from the local chess association office.

Poor Richard. He's so rattled over Topher that he loses a friendly match the next night at the Village chess club. Then it gets worse. He loses his next match in the qualifying rounds for the regional tournament and begins to wonder if he's also losing his mind. Because all he can think about is Topher. What's going to happen when Topher, the perfect prince of the chess world, is found out to be gay? Chess and sexuality do not mix, chess and homosexuality especially. Closeted Richard already has nightmares about being murdered in a hotel room in the Czech Republic or some other place even more barbaric than New York. Aren't there still countries where they have the death penalty for being gay? And are any of them in the international chess federation? Surely they are… Topher's world would come tumbling down if the chess world learned he was…queer.

He's in the all-night drugstore on the corner of his block late one night, staring forlornly at the shelf of sleep aids, when someone speaks to him.

"I thought you might be here."

His blood runs cold at the sound of the young voice behind him. Topher always talks like a lawyer on television, all full sentences, with careful pauses in all the right places. Richard wonders bitterly if it's because he's chess royalty, or if it's the prep school education that makes him talk that way. Or maybe it's just Topher.

"That is, I was hoping I'd find you here, eventually."

He turns to see the demon child himself. Okay, not much of a child anymore—they are pretty much of a height, and Topher must tower over his father now. Richard grits his teeth. Topher was simply not supposed to grow up, or if he was, he was supposed to grow into the role of a geeky brainiac, maybe become a recluse like Bobby Fischer or marry the women's international champion and have a pile of chess genius children. Not grow into a fucking gorgeous Keanu Reeves look-alike. Not grow into a movie idol *who could now beat Richard at chess.*

"You haven't been answering your cell phone," Topher persists.

"I lost it," Richard grunts. He wonders what gave him away, what telltale sign Topher read in his game that told him Richard wasn't spouting homophobic nonsense? There can only be one reason Topher is here, looking for him.

They look at each other for an immeasurable time. Topher seems to be waiting for something. Richard stares into inscrutable eyes and surrenders to the inevitable move: "Do you need a ride somewhere? Would you like to get something to eat?"

Topher merely nods, and his silence is unnerving.

Richard drives them to a restaurant he knows on the West Side—well, to an underground garage nearby, anyway, as one must put the car somewhere. He finds himself not at all surprised that Topher seems in no rush to open the door.

Topher's hand is on his sleeve, in fact. "I don't want to presume, but I have a request."

"But you presume anyway," Richard says, voice low and tired, betraying not a hint of the painful excitement squeezing his heart. It's rather like the heat of a title match, the oppressively charged atmosphere around the black-and-white board, so small and yet with all attention focused upon it. He looks sidelong at Topher. Topher is the one who opened this gambit; it is his move. Richard waits.

"I am sure you will tell me no if I am wrong and you don't want to," Topher says, manners impeccable as always.

Richard huffs. "What's the request?"

"Kiss me," Topher says, and Richard is not prepared for how those two words knock gravity askew. He is spinning in free fall, vertigo threatening to make up into down and east into west.

Best to just do as he asks, then, and Richard anchors himself by pulling Topher to him roughly, his hands yanking the collar of his shirt and nearly cutting his own lip on Topher's teeth. The kiss is pure pleasure, though, the taste of Topher eerily familiar, as if this has happened before, even though it hasn't.

Perhaps Richard has imagined this moment more times than he would ever admit.

When he releases Topher, the poor boy's lower lip is bruised, his pants are visibly too tight, and he has a glazed look in his eye that says he's forgotten entirely where he is.

But not who he's with. "Richard…"

If they are going to play this game, Richard needs to establish his dominance, display his experience, emphasize the gulf between them. At least, that is what he tells himself. Otherwise, he'll never gain any advantage. "Kiss me in return," he demands.

Topher nods, then shifts in the bucket seat until his knees are folded under him and his hands are cradling Richard's face. His ever-serious young eyes lock on to Richard's for a long moment before they close, as he brushes his mouth across the older man's expectant lips.

Richard thinks his head might explode. Topher brushes past

again, then presses more firmly, the tip of his tongue darting into Richard's mouth. Topher is all tightly trammeled desire, as intoxicating and potent as gin and vermouth.

"You're trying so hard to get it right," Richard chides.

Topher jerks back, stung. "You didn't like it?"

"Are you going to be like this the whole time? If I let you get in bed with me, will it be like this?"

"Like what?"

"Like you're ballroom dancing and trying not to make a misstep. If I want that, I can pay for it."

Topher's confidence falters. "But... I mean..." Then he gathers himself to make a countermove. "Well, maybe you should make love to me, then. And show me how it's done."

Richard seizes him by the back of the collar, pulling him close again into another crushing, bruising kiss. "I will shatter you like a window in a hurricane if you're too stiff, you know," he says, and feels Topher stiffen even more at the comment. Richard knows it's cruel to wind him up, but he's unable to help himself.

Topher nods, then squeaks, "Here?"

Richard looks around the inside of the car as if seriously considering it. Then he unlocks the doors. "Hmm, no. Come on."

Topher trails slightly behind his...what. Rival? Intended partner? He doesn't have a word for what Richard is right now. Richard is the former student of Topher's father, and two months ago if you'd asked Topher what his plan was concerning losing his virginity, Richard wouldn't have even come up. But one takes what opportunities the game presents. Richard is perfect and he doesn't even know how perfect.

Topher's confidence wavers some as they walk, though. Are they actually going somewhere to eat first? Was that only a pretense?

Then he sees a sign in a window that makes him think there's a chess club in the building ahead, but no, they couldn't possibly be going to...? No. They walk right past, into the lobby of a somewhat rundown building. Paying for the parking?

But Topher is wrong again. It's a hotel. Richard hands his credit card to the receptionist, who doesn't even take her eyes off the small TV on her desk as she hands it back with a key card.

They ride a noisy elevator up to the fifth floor. Richard leads the way to a room where everything is beige and peach, even the artwork bolted to the wall over the bed. *At least everything looks clean,* Topher thinks. Richard sheds his jacket, draping it on the dresser and then stands, legs slightly spread, by the large bed. He unbuttons his shirt, and is taking off his watch when Topher realizes he's just been staring, watching Richard undress and not doing anything himself.

"I, um..."

"This was your idea, Topher," Richard points out. "Wasn't it?"

"Well, yes," Topher agrees. "I'm just...not sure what to do from this point forward."

Richard sets his watch aside. "Come undress me, then."

Topher takes a breath, correctly divining that this is a test of some kind. Testing his resolve, perhaps. That's what he thinks when he has finished pulling Richard's undershirt over his head and is undoing his belt and unzipping his fly. The *thing* he feels, then sees, so long and hard it has pushed up through the waistband of Richard's underwear, makes him swallow and quaver.

He pulls Richard's pants down anyway, folds them with a neat crease over the jacket, and then looks at the man in front of him. His cock is a proud, red, artful curve away from his body. Topher pets his balls the way one would an imposing dog.

"You have a very determined look in your eye," Richard

says. He climbs onto the bed, leaving Topher standing. He props himself up on pillows, one hand idly moving his foreskin up and down his shaft. "Your turn to undress. Go on."

Topher is mindful of the ballroom dance comment, but he can't just toss his clothes aside and leap onto the bed like a twink from the one porn video he's seen. He takes off his clothes methodically, folds each piece and makes a neat stack on the seat of the desk chair. That's who he is, and this tryst isn't going to change that.

When he looks up at Richard, it's clear that he has found this performance every bit as arousing as some fake slutty strip-tease—maybe more. Topher climbs onto the bed, then sits back on his heels, his own prick bobbing in his lap. "I want this to go well," he says. "As I said before, I think maybe you should lead the dance."

Richard Partridge is entranced by the beauty of the young man climbing onto the bed. Maybe Topher growing up wasn't so bad after all. And surely this can't be Topher's first time? First time with someone older and more experienced, probably.

Richard lingers over the sight of Topher naked, far more entrancing than he had imagined. Not that he had spent much time imagining such a thing. Of course not. Richard resolves that whether this goes well or badly, he will take Topher shopping to replace the too-small suit and whatever else his mother has sent him off to college with that needs replacing.

Yes, he is thinking ahead, but that is the way Richard nearly always thinks. And he knows Topher does, too. That is what chess players do. They learn the rules, then immediately predict what the rules will allow them to do.

He decides to frame everything for Topher in terms he'll understand.

"The winning state here, if we may be claiming there is a single winning state to be defined," Richard says quietly, "is to get my cock into you, for you to come while it's there, and for me to come shortly after that, if not at the same time, which might happen but is hardly necessary. There's no loser in this game, unless you don't enjoy yourself."

Topher nods, as if Richard has just analyzed the checkmate in a junior match.

"You could try kissing me again," Richard suggests. "You might be less stiff now that we're out of the car."

"All right."

Topher crawls over him, lying atop the length of him as he brings their mouths together. His cock nestles into the curve of Richard's hip, and Richard's cock presses against his belly. This kiss ends up necessarily more sloppy as Richard's hands clamp on to Topher's backside, pulling him against him, knocking their noses together. For all the neat words he's used to describe what they're about to do, what he hasn't told Topher is just how much he fucking *needs* him now, and maybe there are no words to describe this need, and the only way to tell it is to just pull at him like he wants to merge their skins together.

Topher loses himself in the kissing and rutting for a while, in the incredible sensation of Richard's skin against his, then suddenly finds himself struggling to get away, to stop the inevitable flood of come from his prick, squirting hot and sudden between their bellies as he cries out, distressed, even as Richard holds him even tighter against him.

"It's all right," Richard croons. "You can come. You'll be ready again in no time, I'm sure." Now that he thinks about it, Richard's been saying that for a few minutes, but words had ceased reaching Topher.

"But now we're all…" Topher's blush is so deep it makes his face even redder than Richard's cock.

"Get a towel from the bathroom and clean us up."

Topher does as suggested, still breathless from the orgasm and the kissing, retrieving a small towel and wiping himself with it. When he returns to the bed, Richard has brought brightly colored packets of condoms and two small tubes of lubricant into the bed. Topher's throat goes dry with anticipation.

He's really going to do this. Finally do this.

He uses the towel to wipe off the semen smeared on Richard's skin, and then follows Richard's gestures to lie on his back.

"For someone who's just come, you're rather tense," Richard says, as he tears the tip off one of the tubes of lube and slicks his fingers with it. "This is supposed to be fun, remember?"

"I'm sorry," Topher says. "I'm just nervous."

Richard revises his estimate of Topher's experience level downward again. *He's embarrassed by smeared come?* He rubs a warm hand over Topher's now clean belly. Topher's eyes mist over as Richard's fingertips just barely brush the boy's soft shaft, which is already hardening again. "You may feel we are playing a game, but there is no winner or loser here," he says, voice low. "There is also no getting it right or getting it wrong, unless one of us isn't enjoying ourselves."

"I'm sor—"

"No apologizing! If you're not enjoying yourself, I need to work a little harder." He rubs his slick fingers between Topher's asscheeks, making no attempt to penetrate, purely teasing. He is gratified to feel Topher's hips rock toward the touch rather than away from it. He teases one small nipple between his lips and enjoys the sigh that elicits.

"How did you know I would like that?" Topher asks breathlessly, when Richard has relinquished his hold on the nub and is now just running a finger over it lightly.

"A good guess," Richard says. "I like it, so I thought maybe you would, too."

"Oh." Richard watches Topher's eyes light up, as if he can see the wheels of logic turning in his head. Yes, logic can be applied to sex, if not quite so rigidly as it is applied to chess. "And do you like..." The pause is just long enough for Topher's cheeks to flush again. "Being penetrated?"

"Not especially," Richard says dryly, but he curves the tip of his finger so that it just barely breaches the boy's tight hole. "I suppose we shall find out if you do?"

"Y-yes..." Topher sucks in a deep breath like he's trying to relax, but utterly failing. And he goes completely rigid when Richard slips a slick finger deeper into him, but the sound he makes isn't one of pain or fear; it's of intense lust. Richard feels the vibration of it in his own groin.

He crooks his finger, stroking Topher on the inside and watching his reaction carefully. It would appear that motion sets off a ripple of pleasure, and Topher groans again.

It is a hungry sound. All indications are that, yes, Topher likes being penetrated.

"I'm adding a second finger," Richard says, "but I won't try it with my cock until you ask me to."

Topher blinks and looks up at the stucco ceiling. *Ask?* He has no idea how to tell if he's ready, so he waits until the fingers drilling into him move freely and both tubes of lube are emptied. And then he tries to think of the appropriate words to say. *I want you?* He supposes there is a certain kind of passion in supplication, he's just not sure he can bring himself to actually beg.

And Richard didn't say beg, he said *ask*.

Topher decides to go for the practical. "In my fantasies, I'm usually on all fours. Can we do it that way?"

"If you like. Why don't you start lying flat on the bed, though? Just shift this pillow under your hips."

Topher moves into position, but he asks, "Why?"

"The penetration will be a little shallower this way. Once you're used to it, if you want, I can lift you up to all fours."

"Ah." He wants to ask, but he has a suspicion that the question is a foolish one and merely asking it might embarrass him so badly he won't be able to look Richard in the eye again. He wants to ask how big Richard really is, comparatively speaking, and whether that's going to make a difference.

"I'm going to put just the tip in, Topher," Richard says, and Topher twists his head to look back and sees that Richard's hand is wrapped around his condom-covered cock so only an inch of it, not even the whole head, protrudes from his fist. He pushes the head of his cock between Topher's cheeks, pressing rhythmically, until at last he pushes in, then pulls out quickly, again and again, until Topher actually tries to push back onto him. Richard lets more of it penetrate on each thrust until he finally lets go of his cock and lets it slide all the way in, his balls coming to rest against Topher's ass.

Topher has clawed the beige bedcovers into a small mountain range, yet feels a sense of triumph. That feeling only grows as Richard begins to fuck, pulling back and thrusting forward, and making ripples of pleasure cascade all through Topher's body.

And Richard, though he has longed for this moment of consummation for longer than he'll admit but at least since that moment when he shook Topher's hand across that chessboard with the cameras clicking, is thrown into a trance of lust so deep, he barely feels his own body other than his cock. Everything is Topher, as his hands skate along Topher's damp ribs, find the curve of his hips, the taste of his sweat at the base of his neck, the scent of him. He loses his sense of himself utterly as he is swallowed by the presence of the young body under him, quite suddenly ready, beyond any rational thought, to pledge himself, to make ridiculous and sentimental pronouncements, to promise to go to whatever lengths to please him....

He has lost his mind. But it feels so damn good he doesn't care.

Topher is overwhelmed with sensation: the damp warmth of the bedcovers under him, Richard's firm weight atop him, the sweet heat of Richard's breath and most of all the relentless cock drilling into his body. It is everything he hoped sex would be. He comes with a shudder, biting down on the urge to cry out, and it is not like any other orgasm he has had, humping his mattress at home or spilling into the fingers of some boy in a restroom. Richard's cock seems to push it out of him from within, and the world goes white.

When Richard pulls at his hips, getting him to all fours, he cannot lift his head. Instead he lifts his ass in what must surely look like a wanton presentation and cries out in surprise as Richard's next thrust is deeper than before, then deeper again, Richard barely slowing his pace, pushing again and again.

As Richard comes close to his own climax, he reaches under Topher, only to find sticky skin and a soft cock. "Ah," he says, understanding the hair trigger of an eighteen-year-old, even if he feels a vague sense of disappointment. Perhaps there will be other chances, perhaps he will teach Topher to last longer....

He shakes his head, trying to reassert rational thinking, but that will not happen until adequate blood flow is restored to his head. All his blood is in his cock, and he fucks Topher hard in his rush to finish. At this angle Topher's back is long and lean, and Richard wants to own every inch of its skin. He bellows as he comes, crushing Topher once more, this time with his arms around his rib cage as he bears him flat to the bed and finishes in him with a last flurry of thrusts.

They lie panting until Topher makes a sound like he is trying to speak. Thinking perhaps he might be trying to say that Richard is too heavy, Richard pulls out and rolls to the side. He's going soft but the condom stays on the bulb of his head, still full of jism. Topher puts a hand on Richard's shoulder. Richard turns to see one glistening eye watching him from under strands of black hair hanging like fringe on a pillow. He brushes back the boy's hair, lock by lock, until he is looking at the absolutely most beautiful face he has ever known—or desired. *Did he always think that? Or is it the sex?* He isn't sure.

"Topher…"

He longs to hear Topher whisper back dreamily *Richard, baby*, or some sweet nothing like that. If he does, Richard will shower him with kisses.

Topher's eye closes and he takes a long breath, then lets it out slowly. Richard can almost feel him thinking.

His eye opens again. "Thank you. I'm glad I picked you to be the first."

Topher's words sting. But he can't pull away. He strokes glossy black hair and says nothing, though inside he is thinking, *And who will be second? Have you calculated that far ahead in the game, Topher Lin?*

The next one will probably be some college student. Now that Topher is over the pesky virginity thing, he'll probably get some boyfriend on campus. Besides, it isn't as if an affair or a relationship between Richard and Topher can exist. Richard tries to imagine the reaction of Master Lin to the news and decides ritual suicide wouldn't be enough to redeem them. A single tryst is easy enough to hide; an ongoing relationship, shared love even...not so easy. And the scandal...it would ruin them both, surely.

But he has to know. In chess terms, he's already made himself vulnerable by moving so aggressively, so now is the time to commit to his strategy. He is proud of how calm his own voice sounds as he asks, "Are you thinking just the once, then?"

Topher's eye closes again. "I...I know this will shock you, but, I had not thought beyond about five minutes ago. Now, I don't know."

"Don't know what?" Richard presses.

Topher rolls onto his back and looks up at him. "Kiss me," he says, holding out his arms. "I'll figure the rest out later."

Richard almost leaps onto him, with a mind to devour him again, but he pauses instead and brushes his lips gently over Topher's, his tongue darting to taste him and his breath teasing him until Topher is the one who surges up, hungry again.

When he falls back, hair spread around his head like a fan, he seems to have come to some conclusion. Richard awaits the pronouncement of his fate.

"There's more there," Topher says, a small frown on his face as if Richard is a particularly interesting yet difficult puzzle. "I'm not done. There's *more*."

The repetition shouldn't make what he means any clearer, yet it does. Richard's heart thumps painfully against his chest. Topher Lin is not done with him as a lover. There's more to explore together. Never mind that Richard wants to stay in the closet, avoid scandal and win the chess world championship. Right now the fact that he can smell Topher's skin is far more important. "There are more firsts, too," he says, voice low.

"Good." Topher lets out a long sigh. "I'm sleepy. Can we sleep here?"

Richard nods. They have the whole night if they want it. He urges Topher under the covers, ignores the fact that they are both less than clean and tosses the condom onto the floor—half the advantage of a hotel room is that someone else cleans up. Topher curls next to him, skin to skin.

Maybe, Richard thinks as he buries his nose in Topher's hair, *maybe by the time Topher is done with me, I'll be ready to be done with him.* It doesn't seem likely, but right at this moment he is far too happy for pessimism. He has lost his mind to beauty and the boy, and it is wonderful.

THE CREAM
IN HIS COFFEE

Eric Del Carlo

I wasn't watching what I was doing and so ended up pouring scalding water on the toe of my left sneaker. I yelped and hopped around like an idiot until the first searing wave passed.

What was distracting me from my important duties at the coffee shop? Juan had walked in: Juan, Juan, beautiful mahogany-skinned Juan.

I had the worst of crushes on him. My infatuation with the muscle-bound Latino was entering its third week, but I had yet to speak to him other than to ask, "You want me to leave room for cream?" when he came to the counter to order his fortifying morning cup of java. I'd only learned his name when I overheard somebody hail him on the street.

Juan worked construction, I assumed—the heavy tool belt and hard hat tucked under his arm gave credence to my theory. I couldn't bring myself to actually ask, afraid my voice would tremble, or he'd see the hard-on that sprang to life the minute he came in the door. I only saw him in the early mornings. He'd set his gear and his newspaper on a small table in the shop's front corner, get his coffee from me and spend about twenty minutes reading the headlines and the sports page before slipping wordlessly out. I spent those twenty minutes furtively ogling him with feverish eyes.

He was just under six feet tall. His physique was ideal, something out of mythology—cannonball shoulders, thick chest, corded biceps, firm thighs and the tightest, most mouthwatering ass I'd ever seen on any male. He had a dense head of the blackest hair, smoldering dark eyes and features that had been molded by God himself to reflect everything in the world that was beautiful. He was in his midtwenties, at least three or four years older than me.

And his skin...it was the shade of varnished wood, of rich chocolate, with a luscious sheen like glowing bronze. I longed to lave it with my lips and tongue, to caress it with my fingers, to marvel at its texture, which I imagined was silky and smooth and hot with his living heat.

I upset a tray of walnut muffins but managed to catch it before any hit the floor. With unsteady hands I set it back on the counter. My fearsome hard-on made my movements awkward.

From the front corner Juan glanced up, dark eyes pinning me briefly. I smiled at him in embarrassment. The corner of his mouth turned up ever so slightly. My insides turned to jelly.

It wasn't that I was cock starved. I'd always considered myself too scrawny to be especially attractive, but I never had trouble finding myself a trick on the weekends. But Juan, with his delectable body and exotic skin, made me—a pale, underfed white kid—weak with lust. I was resigned to worshipping Juan from afar, to turning into a bumbling wreck whenever he was around and to jerking off to thoughts of him in my bed. His beauty was out of my league....

I spent the rest of my shift thinking about the tiny smile he'd thrown me, analyzing it for the smallest hint of mutual attraction. By the time I got home late that afternoon I realized I was being completely stupid—not that that kept me from indulging in torrid mental fantasies of writhing against his succulent brown body.

The next morning I opened the shop alone. I like this part of my day. It's quiet, meditative, just me wiping the tables with the burbling coffee machines for company. I usually get there a half hour before opening time.

Today, however, I turned the corner and jerked to a stop. Juan was standing out front, tool belt and hard hat under one arm, looking casually at his newspaper. I forced myself to start walking.

"Little early today?" I said, trying to sound nonchalant.

His beautiful dark eyes rose from the paper. "Yeah. Woke up and couldn't get back to sleep. I got, what, a half hour before you're open?"

I made a concerted effort not to drop my keys as I unlocked the door. It was even more of a struggle to keep my voice steady as I said, "You can come in now...if you want. I always put a pot of coffee on for myself when I get here."

He smiled, eyes still focused on my face. He followed me inside. The shop's front blinds were down.

I was facing away, which helped to hide my hard-on. I was also trying frantically to evaluate the moment, again reading a hundred different meanings into the situation, desperately hoping that somehow I could finally get my hands on him—and at the same time sure it would never happen.

I was just a few steps inside when Juan answered my multiple questions. From behind, he grabbed a cheek of my ass and gave it a steely-fingered squeeze. Air rushed out of my lungs.

"You got a nice butt for a skinny white guy."

I craned my head slowly around. He was smiling again, gleaming white teeth flashing from between soft brown lips. I tried to speak.

Again he saved me the trouble. He dropped his tool belt and hard hat on a nearby table, turned my body around and planted a kiss on my shocked lips. For what seemed like a long while I was unable to return the kiss I'd been longing for; then, my mouth finally melted, and our lips mashed together. His were as soft as I'd imagined. His moist tongue probed my mouth, encountering my own. We frenched long and deep, my eyes drifting shut.

Eventually our mouths parted. "You like it?"

I opened my eyes, thinking I'd never heard a sillier question, and nodded.

"You want to go in back somewhere?" Juan asked.

With the blinds down we were invisible from the street. "Right here's fine," I said breathlessly. I wanted him so badly. There were only a half-dozen tables out on the floor. Customers mostly got their coffees, cappuccinos and pastries to go.

Our mouths crushed hungrily together again. This time Juan's hands moved over my body, stroking my bony flanks, reaching again for my ass. After a second's hesitation my hands rose to his broad, well-rounded shoulders. He was firm beneath my touch, all muscle and sinew. I caressed his arms as they enclosed me. His tongue danced wildly against mine as my hands roved down his back toward his shapely ass. I moaned into his mouth as my fingers finally closed on its luscious swells.

He pulled my T-shirt out of my jeans, drawing it up over my ribs and my aroused nipples. I lifted my arms, and he tugged it over my head. I unbuttoned his denim work shirt with hasty fingers, then helped yank it off him.

We gazed at each other. His unclothed torso was a wonder

to behold—firm pecs capped by the dark swollen circles of his nipples, classic washboard abs, veins prominent along his muscular arms. And dark, gorgeous flesh...

He was looking at me with the same sort of longing—which in a distant corner of my mind I found rather perplexing. I only weigh about one thirty-five, and while there's not an ounce of fat on me, there's not much in the way of muscle either. Nonetheless Juan's gaze mirrored the rapture in my own eyes.

He lifted a hand and trailed it delicately over my shallow chest, fingertips straying across my left nipple. Imitating him, I stroked his impressive pectorals, my fingers lovingly cupping the solid mounds, trapping a nipple between two knuckles and squeezing.

We explored each other's bodies for several leisurely minutes, our movements strangely synchronized: as my palm glided across his rippling abdominals toward his crotch, Juan's hand slid across my less-defined stomach toward my denim-trapped hard-on.

His hand closed around my blatant bulge and I shivered sweetly. I groped his thick meat through the fabric of his jeans. He jammed his crotch hard against my palm, his cock pulsing.

We removed the rest of our clothing, dropping it carelessly to the floor. I eyed the clock: fifteen minutes until I had to open. It would be enough time.

Naked, we studied each other again. Juan was a solid pillar of masculine strength, legs bowed slightly, body radiating health and stamina. His cock was a gorgeous length of firm meat, the same color as the rest of his stained-wood flesh.

Why he was looking back at me—*me*—with the same lustful leer, I couldn't imagine.

We stepped toward each other and kissed again, each seizing the other's cock. His naked body felt glorious against mine, his dark flesh as smooth as I'd fantasized.

Gasping, I broke my mouth away from his. "I want to suck you," I panted. I prayed he'd had the foresight to bring along condoms.

He had. He fished one out of the pocket of his discarded jeans. I snatched it, tore open the packet and slid it over his cock, then dropped to my knees. My mouth watered in anticipation. His dark-haired balls hung heavily, and it was these I went after first. I moistened the sac with my tongue, lapping in long, savoring strokes. Then I gently sucked one, then the other into my mouth, squeezing them delicately with my lips, drawing in their flavor. Juan moaned above me.

I shifted on my knees, ignoring the discomfort of the hardwood floor, and turned my attention to his cock. I first licked the sides of the hefty shaft, then moved toward the dark jewel of his cockhead.

I held his moist balls in one hand and the column of his hard thigh in my other. I closed my lips around the tip of his cock, setting my tongue loose again. Then I lowered my mouth, letting his impressive length fill me. My tongue curled wildly around his shaft as his head approached the back of my mouth. I felt a muscle jump along Juan's thigh beneath my hand. I swallowed him down to the base, his dense black pubic hairs brushing my cheeks and distended lips.

"That's good..." I heard from above.

I drew my cheeks in tightly and sucked in earnest, picking just the right tempo and increasing it every thirty seconds or so until my mouth was plunging up and down in a blur.

His hips thrust forward, matching the speed of my blow job. As he face-fucked me, his body quivered, then trembled harder.

"Here it comes!" he yelled.

His balls moved beneath my fingers and started unloading, heavy gushes through his shaft, cum filling the condom. I kept my mouth on him until, his leg spasming where I held it, he disengaged himself from my lips. The filled condom fell to the floor, heavy with its load.

I rose to my feet, my cock still rigid. Without hesitation Juan moved into position, settling to his knees, sliding another condom onto my shaft.

I gazed down, dazed with lust, as his mouth closed over me. I put my hands to his broad shoulders to steady myself as he swallowed me, my inches disappearing between his soft lips. His agile tongue slithered up and down my cock, sending hot jets of pleasure through my thin, pale body.

He looked so beautiful kneeling before me, strong hands gripping my skinny thighs, his dark-haired head bobbing faster and faster. He was an expert cocksucker, taking my length effortlessly, laughing off his gag reflex and burying his nose in my pubic curls.

Juan moved one hand from my leg to my balls, cupping my sac and squeezing gently. My excitement was mounting by rapid degrees, and soon his mouth was racing up and down my cock, lips wrapping me tightly, fingers urgently trying to milk my cum from my balls.

He didn't have long to wait. My eruption approached, my flesh tingling, my fingers digging into the solid mounds of his shoulders. I rose slightly up onto my toes and let loose. Cum hammered out of me, Juan's mouth clamped tightly around my shaft, his tireless tongue still squirming all over my cock. My eyes closed again as the waves of fulfilled lust crashed over me.

When I was done, I opened my eyes and looked vaguely at the clock on the wall. I had to open the coffee shop in three minutes. Still I took the time—not caring if those first customers got their caffeine fixes—to give Juan another deep, lingering kiss.

He grinned at me. "Y'know, it's probably not politically correct to say this but...I've always had this thing for skinny white guys."

I laughed. "Well, we've all got our kinks, don't we?"

BOOKENDED BY BEAUTY

Jamie Freeman

I fell asleep with my iPod on last night, *Spring Awakening* blasting in an endless loop while I floated up into the shimmering sunlight of purple summer. It reminds me of the summer I turned fifteen and spent the afternoons sleeping under emerald leaves at my uncle's farm, the sun beating down through the foliage, my headphones blasting *Chess* over and over. I listened and listened, flipping the cassette over again and again until the tape clicked and dragged. I floated out of myself then as well, fleeing into the music. I remember that feeling so clearly; as if the music itself was lifting me up, up away from my father's quietly restrained, meticulously ordered little world into the freedom of the dancing sun-streaked maple trees. And last night I felt my body rising sunward like it did so many years ago.

Nick thinks I need to spend a little more time inside myself and a little less time inside my show tunes. Last night he left Jennifer's card on the table with a yellow Post-it that said, *Appointment*. Jennifer's my shrink. Nick's not a subtle guy; he used to teach high school English, so he sometimes likes to provide me with life lesson plans in the form of suggestive words scrawled on Post-it notes. Sometimes he leaves a checkerboard of them on the refrigerator spelling out a variety of possible solutions like a two-dimensional Rubik's Cube. One afternoon I spent an hour shuffling Post-its from place to place; over dinner I told Nick I thought I was going to buy a pool. He stared at me for a long time, dropped his fork onto his plate, slid his chair back from the table and said, "Fuck you, you stupid asshole. That Post-it said *poll.*" He wanted me to poll our friends about vacation destinations, but sometimes the lessons we learn are not in the lesson plan.

Now every morning before his beauty regimen, Nick swims laps in the pool I bought that year, maintaining long, slender limbs and a hard, perfect stomach. He learned to love the pool and he polled our friends himself, planning our cruise to Mexico and dragging me along with a suitcase full of sunscreen, books and reluctance.

"Poll, my ass," I yelled after him that night as he stormed down the hall.

The lesson plan for last night was directing me to make an appointment with my shrink, who I haven't seen in a couple of months. I think seeing her now would be a waste of money. No need for professional intervention, just look at a fuckin' calendar. Anyone else would see that the neatly numbered squares lead inexorably toward my fortieth birthday. But Nick thinks age-related anxiety's bullshit since he didn't have a freak-out when he rolled past forty. Honestly, if I looked as good as he did, I'd roll on past without a thought. But I don't. I'm gaining weight in all the places forty-year-olds do. I still have my runner's legs and I swim in the afternoons to try to even things out, but it's a losing battle. And my thick, beautiful chest hair is growing long and kinky and colonizing my shoulders and my back. And I've never had a beautiful face to offset the normalcy of my body. I fuckin' hate gettin' old.

There are fifty-one days until I turn forty.

Nick's in the bathroom now, pouting in front of the mirror where he spends an hour each morning, his delicate, long-fingered hands competently slowing his beauteous decline. I'm still in bed with the covers kicked off in the Florida heat, but I can picture him there, his face damp from the first rinse as he smoothes a five-hundred-dollar cleansing cream across his beautiful pale cheeks. He's gently rubbing the lines from his face like he's Photoshopping his skin, perfecting perfection, airbrushing Rock Hudson.

I usually walk into the bathroom at the end of his rituals, kiss him on the cheek or massage his shoulders for a minute or two, and then join him in the shower. This morning I look over his shoulder into the mirror, still transfixed by his beauty after nearly fifteen years, and I wonder what he can possibly see there to elicit such methodical, pathological—Jennifer might say obsessive-compulsive—concern on his part. He is flawlessly beautiful, a truly stunning man, entering his prime at forty-five, when I've already left mine far behind me.

I kiss a ticklish spot on his neck, letting my sandpaper chin scrape against his smooth skin.

"You fell asleep with your iPod on again," he tells me.

I run a hand through my hair, pulling on the silver curls, glancing up from beneath my thick eyelashes, posing like the subject of an old George Hurrell portrait, all drama and lighting and archetypal beauty. I was once told I looked like a young Burt Lancaster, all curly hair, broad cheeks and cocksucking lips, the way he looked in *The Killers* with Ava Gardner. My lips pout, but I can't hold on to the moment. I break into a grin. I feel overweight and hairy and apelike in his presence. I do a well-worn comic bit, hopping around, arms dangling, body swaying from one foot to the other.

"Oh, monkey," he whispers.

"Me Oliver," I grunt.

Nick's dark eyes open, slow as a morning bloom, and then narrow, watching me in the mirror.

"You need me to shave your back," he says finally. There is an understated smile inching across his lips, the wrinkle damage of such movements minimized by periodic injections of Botox.

I'm naked; my erection slides between the twin globes of his perfect ass. He rubs his puckered hole against me, daring me to enter him. He's always been a wildcat in the sack, willing to do anything, eager to do everything. He's as compartmentalized in his life as the Post-its on the fridge. He's got all these little note-sized worlds: Office, Home, Body, Face, Family, Sex. He will stand worrying about his wrinkles; methodically touching up his hair; peeling and exfoliating his face, his heels, his hands; smoothing everything to porcelain perfection; pulling back when I touch his cheek for fear I will somehow upset the alchemical balance that keeps him youthful and perfect. But then flip to the next Post-it and he's on his knees on the kitchen tile behind me pushing his thumbs into me and rimming out my hole like he's devouring a nectarine, wallowing in the smell of sweat and the salty fruit between my asscheeks. Flip to the next, on which he's written the words *water sports* in neat block letters. He leaves that one on the mirror in the master bathroom one night, then pulls me naked into the cold stone of the shower stall and kneels, grinning and stroking his cock, whispering a string of stinging, sexy profanity as I piss across his stomach and chest and finally his perfect face. A week after the pool-poll thing, he leaves a Post-it note on my pillow that says *Poll my ass* and then moans and thrashes, perfectly manicured fingers smearing oily lube across the sheets and scraping the skin off my arms when I wrestle him onto the mattress, strip off his boxers and plow into him.

Nick's always been direct like that. That's how we ended up with Andy. He left a Post-it that said, *Three's Company Too* next to the coffeepot one morning. We drank the last of the organic blend we bought in Guatemala and started looking at the possibilities.

Now, in the bathroom, he reaches back and gives my cock a nice, slow tug. He turns around, grabbing our cocks together in his hands. They're as opposite as we are. His is long and pale and thin with a small pinkish head. Mine is shorter, thicker, more blunt and bluish, the shaft heavy and veined like a darkly living creature. I lean back against the bathroom wall letting him work me over until I splatter a load of cum all over his hands. He comes right after that, pushing his head against my soft belly, leaving a trail of thin milky cum entangled in my hair. He kneels down and licks us both clean; my skin shudders under his tongue. As the flame of orgasm fizzles and finally drops from the sky above me, a dying flare in the winter sky, the dimming light behind my eyes triggers a memory: the night I first saw Nick.

It was the fall of 1996 and my best friend Jonathan and I were at an amateur production of *Pippin*. When the music died at the end of the finale, a puzzled, uncomfortable silence hung over the room. The pause was so long the cast started to react, faces changing, smiles altering at the corners or behind kohl-lined eyes. When the roar of applause finally arrived, tears of relief wet thespian cheeks.

I watched the relieved actors taking their bows, Pippin still bare-chested and barefoot from the finale in which the other players had stolen away everything but his linen pants, pushing the scenery into the wings, stripping his life down to an empty stage and the stark glare of a single overhead bulb. The actor, Jamie, was laughing now, smiling and waving to the audience, but moments ago his voiced had cracked under the weight of his heartbreaking choice: live your life fast as a supernova or slow as a candle. "Think about the sun, Pippin," sang the chorus. I wanted him to fly, like Icarus into the inferno of an extraordinary life. *Live it for me*, I thought. But as he has done every time I've seen the show, Pippin chose life, domestic and slow and steady.

This show always makes me anxious and peevish.

When the lights came up, we stood and looked in the direction of the greenroom, where we had been promised free wine. We were standing behind a herd of chattering, slightly puzzled theatergoers trying to exit. "What happened at the end?" one woman asked another. "I don't know, it's too artsy for me, with that bare stage and him half nekkid and that lightbulb."

"It was good till then," the first woman said.

Jonathan was bouncing on the balls of his feet, clapping his hands rhythmically, his lips moving as he processed the show's startling finale. He'd been going through this cheerleading phase and everything was converted to a cheer, repeated with hand-claps as punctuation and a few precision arm or leg moves for emphasis. *You might not be an eagle* (clap) *that soars down to the sea* (clap). *But if you're tied to nothing* (clap, arms up). *You're never really free.* (clap, clap)

A fat man in front of us whispered "Faggots," to his wife; I touched Jonathan's hand in an attempt to waylay another cheer, but I was too late. *Love me or hate me* (clap), *you don't have to date me* (clap, clap). We let them move ahead of us, the woman using her wobbling arm and an aluminum cane to leverage herself from one step to the next. Her eyes blazed with anger; her breath was ragged from the exertion of the stairs.

In the greenroom a buffet of cold, unappetizing food had been carefully laid out on gold plastic tablecloths, but the actors were too amped to eat anything, fluttering around the crowded room sweating and giggling and fawning over the handsome Pippin. I'd known Jamie for a couple of years. He reminded me of the old porn star Casey Donovan, with his straight, windswept brown hair and darkly drugged, lost eyes. He looked startled by the attention, shifting his weight from one bare foot to the other, holding a dozen red roses against his finely muscled chest. He was self-consciously pretty. "Strike a pose, girl," I whispered as I passed him.

He shifted his weight to one foot, hips tilting, giving his body an S-shaped twist that showed off his trim form to beautiful effect. He bit his lip to let people know he was having deep thoughts. When he laughed, it was in a singer's voice, controlled and beautiful as if he had never left the stage. I watched him talking to a hunky guy who touched him repeatedly on his bare shoulder. I imagined the two of them naked, the hulking hottie pushing Jamie's head down with meaty fingers and fucking his tiny, curved ass.

"Oh, baby, slide me between those fine buns," Jonathan whispered, arms circling my waist. I laughed.

"You hate it here," he said.

"No, of course not."

"You do," he insisted. "And you hate me for bringing you here."

I turned around and pulled him into a hug.

"I love you, Johnny Boy," I whispered.

"Knock it off, you two." Jonathan's friend Brenda waved us

over to meet her niece, who had played Pippin's love interest, Catherine. She was quite pretty, with plain hair and delicate features. Jonathan and I tossed superlatives at her for a while, watching her smile fade to an uncomfortable mask. I noticed and stopped, but Jonathan kept going. The movement of the crowd gave me vertigo, the pious clucking of the Old Gainesville matrons making me suddenly queasy. I was going to need a drink to survive the next ten minutes.

I found a plastic cup that looked pretty clean and a bottle of merlot that looked pretty cheap and I introduced them. And then I saw Nick: dark-eyed, dark-haired perfection. I literally gasped; my knees felt weak and I thought I was going to throw up. When I told Nick the story later, all he really got from it was that he made me nauseous. For me it was an epiphany of sorts, as if the universe was saying, *Think about the sun, Oliver.* But rather than floating up into his brilliance, I looked down at my shoes, my mouth watering in desperate preparation for vomit. I pressed the palm of my left hand to the wall and tried to breathe.

A woman in a flowered jacket touched me with long pink nails. "Are you all right, honey?"

I nodded.

"Are you choking?"

I looked up at her, startled. "What?"

"They say you're supposed to ask that," she said.

"I'm fine, really," I said, glancing back at Nick.

I felt like my soul was retrieving some past-life memory that would guide me through this moment to make sure I didn't fuck it up. Maybe it's that feeling of recognition that made me afraid to speak to him. What if I fucked it up anyway?

Luckily he was looking away, his eyes sliding up and down Jamie's body, from dark hair to bare feet and back again. He was staring so unabashedly I was getting an erection by proxy, but I couldn't move or stop salivating, so I stood, stiff and still as a statue, watching. I knew if this guy wanted Jamie, he would have him. And I wouldn't stand a chance.

"Honey, you're sure I can't help you?" the flowered lady asked.

"No, really, I'm fine on my own."

"Well, if you say so," she smiled, patting me on the shoulder and gliding away in a lavender-scented cloud.

I looked back at Nick, who had not moved. I studied his crisp beautiful Greek features: dark wavy hair, thick eyebrows, prominent nose and bottomless eyes. He was a pale beauty, his cheeks thin and slightly pink. He had long piano player's hands that extended from the pressed cuffs of his white oxford. I looked at him and knew that he was watching Jamie. I wondered if they would go home together and whether he was a top or a bottom and whether he had a treasure trail to point the way to his hidden charms.

He turned toward me and I pretended to be looking beyond him. He took no notice of me. I blushed and surreptitiously wiped my eyes as I stumbled toward Jonathan's laughter.

He was that beautiful.

We didn't meet that night. Nick went home with Jamie and they fucked semiprivately and fought publicly for a couple of months. Jamie actually introduced me to Nick at his birthday party, grabbing me by the shoulder, pushing me toward Nick and sneering, "You two shits are perfect for each other. Oliver, Nick. Nick, Oliver." He was right, of course, but he could have been kinder about it.

Now, in the bathroom, the air smells like cum and toothpaste. Nick is pulling himself up off the floor, his knees cracking in protest. He grins and shrugs, tossing his head and letting his gorgeous dark hair fall forward over his forehead.

"I smell teen spirit," Andy says from the hall. "You kids started without me."

I glance over at Andy's lean form. He's standing stretched against the door frame, backlit perfection, his body graceful and feline, like the Rum Tum Tugger, all limbs and pelvis and, in Andy's case, cock. He's wearing a tight, pink midriff T-shirt that says SARAH PALIN 2012 in purple letters across the front. And that's it. A trail of flaming ginger hair descends from his navel to the nest of curls that surround the base of his enormous, pendulous cock. His bright pink balls hang loose and low, swinging with his cock like an invitation to the tropics.

Andy sips from an oversized coffee mug.

"Did I get the reference right, Daddy?" He's talking to Nick, who hates it when Andy calls him that. But Andy likes playing the age game, reveling in the indignant look he gets from Nick's beautiful, dark eyes. Andy's tongue slides across his upper lip and his cock starts to move, the girth beneath the loose skin shifting like a python reaching down from a low-hanging branch to snatch a careless finch. I watch it move and feel my own cock growing thick again in response.

"Go fuck yourself, pretty baby," Nick says, leaning into the shower to turn on the jets. Steam starts to rise almost immediately from the cool stone and Nick steps inside, closing the glass door.

"Bitch," Andy says, laughing. "What's up with him?"

"I dunno," I say.

Andy steps into the room, offers me the mug and reaches down to run his fingertips along the base of my cock. His fingers are warm, sliding down between my balls and then along my taint until his fingertip pokes gently at my *rosebud*—his word, not mine. I sip the hot milky coffee and lean back against the wall, letting Andy slide first one, then two and then three fingers inside me.

We met Andy by accident. I got that *Three's Company Too* Post-it, and Nick and I talked a lot about "a third." We batted some rules back and forth, even made a list, but the whole thing seemed absurd. So we agreed to wait and see what happened.

Back when I was single, I used to cruise the bathrooms sometimes. Yeah, yeah, yeah, it's de rigueur to look down on the whole tearoom scene now that iPhones and XTube have made everyone a porn star and nobody seems to give a flying fuck. But in the world before all that, when small-town boys lived in fear of preachers and police and nobody would admit to wanting to be a porn star, even if they'd ordered some VHS tapes from a black-and-white ad in the back of a porno magazine they bought on a trip to Atlanta, when there was a danger and romance to cruising, there was a feeling of empowerment in dropping to your knees on the cold tile floor of a public men's room and sliding your bouncing erection under the partition into the warm adoration of a guy you'd never look twice at in the street. It was hot and scary and crazy and dangerous.

The place I cruised most often was the fourth-floor men's room in the Tan Building on Barrett Drive. Back in the day there were a couple of Gator football players who used to wander in at odd hours and slip their cocks under the partitions to be ravenously fellated by a tenured economics professor with a wedding band and manicured hands, or a tall A/V guy with a ponytail and long, bloodless white fingers. The first time I realized what was going on, I'd followed one of the Gators out of my econ class and down the hall to the men's room. There was something hungry and desperate in his eyes that appealed to me at the time.

I was cute back then, dark eyes, dark hair, a slim lithe body just beginning to sprout the forest of hair that would eventually earn me my monkey sobriquet. I saw Gatorboy go into one of the stalls, fidget and tap a bit and then drop to his knees.

From where I was standing, I could see the soles of his Nikes framing his broad white ass. As he leaned forward I remember watching his asscheeks spread to reveal the pink starburst, winking at me from a thicket of dewy, wispy hair. I imagined myself diving onto the floor, arms outstretched in front of me like an Olympic diver. I could feel the cold tile under my arms and my belly as I slid under the partitions, coming to rest against his sweaty, smelly hole, sliding in there face-first, arms burrowing under him, tongue digging into his puckered hole. I could smell the heavy odor and feel the wet tang of his sweat against my lips, the coarse texture of his hair against my nose. I pulled out my cock and watched him, his ass muscles straining as the cock-sucker worked him. His ass rocked back and forth, winking and winking. I jacked myself faster. A pale hand stretched around his asscheek, a long saliva-slicked finger tracing his pucker. Gatorboy gasped and then groaned as the finger slid inside him, and I came all over the place, shooting three or four feet up into the air in front of me, cum splattering the door of the cubicle closest to me. I must have groaned or something because there was a sudden commotion, Gatorboy jumping to his feet, clothes rustling and then he and I were face-to-face. I was standing there with my cock in my hand, cum still dripping from the head. He looked at me, and then shoved me hard against the wall. "Fuckin' faggot," he snarled.

I slammed against the tile and thought, *That's fuckin' hot.* I was hooked.

* * *

It was in that same bathroom many years later that I met Andy. Like Nick, Andy's a natural beauty, but being from a generation weaned on reality television and *American Idol*—he was fifteen when he watched the first season of that alleged American classic—he understands what his beauty can buy him. He was born into startling wealth, both economic and genetic, and he takes them both eloquently for granted. Nick calls Andy "pretty baby" with a mixture of praise, affection and fear. Andy will turn twenty-four a week before I turn forty. Nick will still be forty-five. Nick worries about our ages more than he should.

Andy, despite his startling beauty and his preternatural self-confidence, is an old soul. He's centered and calm in a way I could never be. He meditates, disdains junk food and spends the afternoons he doesn't have work or classes standing at his easel, painting naked in the sparkling sunlight. Our friends sometimes mistake his complete lack of self-consciousness for feckless innocence, but he's more calculating than that. You can almost imagine him walking naked onto the set of "Real World DC" and conspicuously ignoring the cameras. He has an XTube account, and his library of films has logged over a million views. He's desperate to perform, to be seen, to be praised and to be loved; which brings me, somewhat obliquely, to the circumstances of our meeting.

I was in the Tan Building for a meeting with one of my clients, an old guy who was trying to dodge a sexual harassment charge filed by a slutty sophomore public relations major who'd blown more professors than I had and who probably framed this old bastard because he asked her to turn in a term paper or something. We were meeting in his office to review some pretrial motions and when we finally packed it in, he walked me out into the corridor, shook my hand and ambled back into his hobbit-hole, leaving me standing in a familiar corridor. I could smell paint and mildew as I walked down the hallway toward the men's room. When I pushed open the inner door, I stopped in midstride. Things around me shifted into fast-forward and I struggled to catch up.

Andy was completely naked, his body thick and muscular, forested in ginger hair from his feet to his clavicle, his hands tied to the poles that supported two adjacent stalls, his arms outstretched like Christ on the cross. My cock jolted awake in my suit pants. The ginger Christ was a vision of fiery perfection, his body illuminated by a shaft of sunlight from the window that made his hair shimmer and his skin shine. His legs were spread, his weight perfectly balanced on his broad, high-arched feet. His finely muscled legs rose to thin hips and a tight waist. His broad shoulders branched from a perfect inverted V of muscle that rose from the obstructed region of his crotch past ridged abs, hard bronzed nipples and solid slab-like pecs, all of it covered in a carefully manicured lawn of golden-reddish hair.

His head was bowed, a tousled mass of hair veiling his face. Kneeling in front of him, obstructing my view and noisily worshipping his cock, was an overweight redneck who, when his head whipped around to face me, I recognized as the Gatorboy who had led me into this men's room more than twenty years before. A vertiginous heat crept across my face. He was at least sixty pounds overweight, his Wranglers sagging in the back to reveal his enormous ass, cracked down the center like a massive dumpling. A John Deere ball cap worn backward imperfectly hid his receding hairline, and his angry eyes danced over a graying mustache.

"I told you to fuckin' lock the door," Andy snarled.

"He ain't nobody," Gatorboy said, turning and staggering to his feet.

"Goddammit," Andy shouted, shifting his arms and slipping his makeshift bonds. He rubbed his wrists and watched me, his expression cagey. "Who're you?"

"He ain't nobody," Gatorboy said again.

"Then he must be somebody," Andy said pulling on his jeans, tucking his still-glistening cock inside and reaching for his T-shirt.

"What? You're just gonna fuckin' go now? After I done drove all this way?" Gatorboy watched Andy pull on his running shoes.

"Fuck off, Gary."

"Fuck you, Andy. I'm done with your stupid horseshit." Gatorboy kicked one of the cubicle doors, giving the row of stalls a good shake and then stomped out the door.

"I just came in to piss," I said.

Andy scowled at me, and then reached over and picked up his video camera off the sink. He flicked a switch with his thumb and looked at me, his eyes curious and blue.

He watched me in silence, his breathing even and low. My chest felt tight and I wondered for a moment if I was having a heart attack.

"It's just anxiety, man."

"What?"

"It's just anxiety. You know, the symptoms: breathing, elevated pulse, red face, sweating. You're not having a heart attack. But I might kick your ass for fucking up my shoot."

"Your shoot?" I said, finally getting it. "Fuck you, your shoot."

"That guy was a minister."

"Oh, Jesus."

"Yeah, baby."

"Who the fuck *are* you?" I said, beginning to smile.

"I am the great I am," he said, wrapping the camera strap

around his fingers and dropping the camera to his side. "Wanna
fuck?"

"Can I bring a friend along?"

"Three's company too," he said.

The rest is histrionics, as Jonathan says.

The next two years were transformative and liberating and
scary. I took Andy home that afternoon, and Nick and I fucked
him until we exhausted ourselves. I woke in the middle of the
night to find Andy wearing my *Phantom Der Oper* T-shirt, sitting
on the sofa with his bare legs tucked underneath him, laughing
and watching an old rerun of "The Avengers." *I could love this
boy*, I thought to myself. I padded across the living room naked
and plopped down on the sofa next to him, propping my feet
on the coffee table and dropping my hand onto his thigh. He
reached down and slid his fingers between mine, holding my
hand as we watched the last half of the episode that ends with
Mr. Steed pulling Mrs. Peel in a rickshaw. As the credits rolled,
Andy shifted his body, turning to face me. The smell of sex was
overwhelming. The hair across his left thigh was matted with
dried cum. He smiled when he saw me looking.

"I think that's Nick's," he said.

I leaned down, licked it and nodded. "Yes," I said.

He laughed, the gesture knocking several years off his age.
The man I'd met earlier in the day, hung from the stalls of a
public restroom in mock crucifixion, now looked like a high
school senior. His eyes squinted in merriment, his face stubbled
and shiny in the light from the television. I watched him, trying
not to feel too much.

"It was just a game," he said.

"Can you read my mind?" I asked in my best Margot Kidder
voice.

"Do you know what it is that you do to me?" he replied.

"Oh, Clark, you're such a hunk." A voice from the darkness behind the sofa startled us both.

"Nick." Andy reached up for Nick's hand. Nick laughed and let Andy pull him down on the couch. He was wearing a pair of blue boxers, his hair tousled and his face still partially immobilized by the vestiges of sleep.

I looked at the two of them, my beautiful partner and this new man who had so easily captivated the two of us. I wanted to jump up and run away, never looking back. I also wanted to propose marriage on the spot to the both of them. My compromise was to move around in front of them, take Nick's cock in my mouth and slide my fingers around Andy's. We fucked again on the sofa in front of flickering images of Peel and Steed investigating a voodoo trance in Hertfordshire.

This morning in the bathroom all those tentative moments, fraught with anxiety and newness and uncomfortable silences seem so distant. Andy has become a part of our lives, his own future inextricably intertwined with ours. Nick asked me yesterday if we should ask him to move in with us permanently. *Three's Company Too.*

Andy's fingers move inside my ass, stretching and pushing me in the place he knows will make me drop the mug of coffee. I reach out trying to balance the mug on the counter. He steadies the mug himself and then engulfs my cock with his lips. I can hear the water in the shower pounding the stone tiles like rain in springtime. Nick is singing softly, "Elaborate Lives" from *Aida*; he's as much of a show queen as I am, though he feigns disdain for all musical theater except *Rent*, which he considers too generationally relevant to completely discard.

Andy finds my prostate and his poking sends flashes of

sensation up behind my eyelids like reverse fireworks, blossoms of darkness that blot out my vision. I gasp and come into his mouth, a bursting trickle, really, my reservoir having already been depleted.

He sucks until he's tickling me and I push him away.

He looks up at me from beneath his ginger forelock, eyes deep and blue, liquid as a penitent. I want to offer him the absolution he seeks, but he is the wise one. I touch his cheek. "Arise, my son," he says.

"Thank you, father," I reply, letting my fingertips guide him up to a standing position. He kisses me; his tongue tastes of cum.

"Is anyone else going to shower this morning?" Nick calls above the sounds of the water.

Andy grins and peels off his shirt and steps into the steaming glass and stone cubicle.

I watch his body disappear into the steam.

It's almost midnight when my phone rings. I'm standing naked in the kitchen contemplating a Ziploc bag filled with Oreos. I hear music from the front room. The cast of "Glee" singing "No Air"—Jonathan's personal ring tone. I run into the living room and grab my iPhone from the pile of personal electronics on the bar.

"Hello, gorgeous," he says.

"Hullo, Johnny Boy."

"What's up, Oliver?" he asks.

"Nothing."

"Your message sounded like something."

"I want to Maria von Trapp," I blurt.

"Climb ev'ry mountain, baby" he says, laughing.

"Does it make me a bad person?" I ask, opening the French

doors and stepping naked onto the wooden decking.

"Everyone thinks about running," he says. "But is that what you want?"

"I dunno." I pause. "Where are you?"

"Lame diversion," he says.

"Fuck you," I mumble.

"I'm leaning against my bike looking out over the Bay. It's stunning—sunset here. The sky's fiery, pink and orange over the hills and the ocean. The bridge is red, almost the color of adobe. It's the second-most beautiful place on earth."

"Second?"

"Well, of course there's your place."

I laugh. "My place?"

"Fuck you," he says. He takes a draw from his water bottle. "You're bookended by beauty."

"Don't let your husband hear you talk like that," I say, embarrassed.

"His words, not mine. He's the writer."

"Do you really believe that?" I ask.

"They're among the most beautiful men I've ever known."

"But is it extraordinary?"

"Your life?" He's laughing. "Shit."

"You're killin' me."

"You love it, Oliver. Your house is filled with art; your bed is filled with men; your heart is filled with love. What more could you ask for?"

"Please, sir, I want some more," I say.

"Never before has a boy wanted more," he says, half singing.

I sigh.

"O-M-G! Was that a sigh?"

I sigh again.

He's silent for a moment. "Is that why you called me?"

"No, no, it's not bad—it's just that Nick wants Andy to move in. You know, permanently."

"Girl! Jump! On! That!" Jonathan is shouting; I pull the phone away from my ear.

"Do you think it'll last?"

"Shouldn't you be all don't-rain-on-my-parade instead of the-man-that-got-away?"

"It feels domestic."

"You'll be living with two men in a permanent three-way relationship. It's domestic, but it'd fuckin' kill that Reverend Dobson asshole."

"Maybe," I say.

"Think about the sun, Oliver," he says.

"That's what I'm doing."

"Did it ever occur to you that life with Nick and Andy *is* the sun and rejecting them is rejecting something extraordinary? Good metaphors work both ways."

This stumps me.

"The sun's slipping lower now, Oliver; almost gone below the horizon."

I imagine what he's seeing, the incendiary pinks and oranges draining from the sky.

"It's gone," he says, his voice soft, resigned.

When I get off the phone, Nick is asleep in Andy's arms in front of the TV. Andy is watching Jack Tripper fall over the back of the couch and laughing like it's the funniest thing he's ever seen. I lean over the back of the sofa and kiss him.

"So tell me, beautiful, when are you moving in for good?"

TIDES

Michael Bracken

Jamie and I were the only people on the white-sand beach, and we didn't notice the lone swimmer until he walked out of the Caribbean wearing nothing at all.

My cock stirred at the sight and I blinked. Twice.

Jamie nudged me. "Do you see what I see?"

"So, I'm not imagining it?"

"If you are," he said, "then I'm having the same fantasy."

The sun-bronzed swimmer finger-combed his long black hair away from his face. The motion of his powerful arms made his broad chest expand and his already-tight abdomen constrict. His thick, uncut phallus and heavy scrotum hung from a dark nest between his thighs, and there was no evidence at all that the warm Caribbean water had caused shrinkage. I had never in my life seen a man so perfect.

"They didn't say anything about *this* in the brochure," Jamie said. "I think there would be more men on this beach if they had."

We had come to the island during spring break to get away

from the repressive Baptist university where we were enrolled as sophomores and had booked ourselves into a little-known, out-of-the way place with few of the amenities the expensive resorts on the far side of the island offered. The best things our two-room cottage had going for it were the secluded white-sand beach, the sea view and the privacy that would allow us the opportunity to explore each other at leisure. The trip was Jamie's idea, and he'd paid for everything. He thought it would be good for our relationship to get away from the university.

Jamie and I couldn't take our eyes off the naked swimmer, though, and we watched as he walked north along the shoreline until he disappeared from view. As if in a daze, the swimmer never acknowledged us nor ever acted as if he knew we were present.

I leaned over. "If my cock was any harder," I whispered in Jamie's ear, "I could pound nails with it."

"Do you want to go back to the cottage?"

Of course I did, and it wasn't long before we stripped off our flip-flops and board shorts.

Jamie and I have been together since the day we met during freshman orientation, one blond gravitating toward another with the knowledge that we shared something our classmates didn't—something that would likely get us expelled if it became common knowledge—and during the eighteen months or so we had been together we had discovered each other's likes and dislikes.

As soon as we had stripped off our board shorts and tank tops, I sat on the side of the bed and Jamie knelt between my widespread thighs. He cupped my balls in his hand and took the swollen head of my cock in his mouth. He spanked it with his tongue and then licked away the precum that oozed from the pee slit. As he kneaded my nuts together, he slowly took more of my cock into his mouth until he had swallowed about two-thirds of it. Then he drew his mouth back until his pearly white teeth caught on the spongy soft ridge of my glans. He did it again and again, covering my shaft with his saliva, never quite taking all of me down his throat.

Jamie wrapped his free hand around his erect cock and began tugging at it, jerking off as fast as he could. All the while he continued his oral assault on my erection. Jamie came first—he usually does—spewing spunk on my shin, the bedspread and the carpet. By then I was nearing release. I grabbed the back of Jamie's head, threading my fingers through his short, blond hair and pulling his head down as I thrust my hips upward, slapping his chin with my balls and sinking my cock so deep it triggered his gag reflex.

I came hard, firing hot spunk against the back of Jamie's throat as I released my grip on his head, allowing him to pull back so that he could swallow every drop of my cum.

After he had swallowed and had licked my cock clean, Jamie rose from the floor and settled onto the bed next to me. "Seeing that guy come out of the water really turned you on, didn't it?"

I had been with other guys before Jamie, and I had been with other guys since meeting Jamie—though he didn't know about any of them—and I knew I had to tread carefully. "He was nice to look at," I admitted, "but he isn't you."

Jamie and I saw the swimmer later that evening when we went to a beachside bar a mile from our hotel, a place that was little more than a roof with corner supports, a bar at one end and a dozen tables at the other. He had dressed in a floral print shirt, khaki shorts and leather sandals, but it was difficult to look at him without remembering all the sun-bronzed skin we had seen earlier that afternoon. He sat alone, drinking shot after shot of whiskey as he stared out at the water.

Jamie and I sat at the bar nursing piña coladas, sharing funny stories about our past that wouldn't have been funny if we had been sober and swapping spit every so often, not caring one whit what our bar mates—mostly locals—thought about our public display of affection. Even though I was with Jamie, I kept glancing at the swimmer. Finally, after enough drinks had given me the courage, I pushed myself off the bar stool and made my way to where he sat.

"Hey," I said.

He looked up and I realized he had at least fifteen years on us.

"We saw you this afternoon." I indicated Jamie, who was gripping the bar tightly to keep from falling off his stool. "On the beach."

He said nothing.

"Hob lay gringo?" I slurred. "Polly voo American?"

"I speak English." He had a deep voice, like Darth Vader without the respirator.

"We saw you drinking alone," I continued. "We thought you might like company."

The swimmer glanced at Jamie and then returned his attention to me. He kicked the chair across from him out from under the table and it slid backward a good three feet. "So sit."

As I sat, I motioned for Jamie. He staggered over with our drinks and dropped onto the chair to my left.

"I'm Kyle," I said. "This is Jamie."

The swimmer saw that our glasses were nearly empty, so he caught the heavyset waitress's attention and indicated with a circular wave of his index finger that he wanted a round of drinks. She waddled away.

Because the swimmer had yet to introduce himself, I asked, "And you are?"

He stared at his empty shot glass for a moment and then said, "Jack. Just call me Jack."

I said, "Good thing you aren't drinking Shirley Temples."

Jamie giggled. He'd matched me drink for drink but he couldn't handle his liquor.

When the waitress returned, Jamie reached for his wallet because he always paid when we were together. He had a trust fund and I only had a Pell grant. Jack put one hand on Jamie's forearm and stopped him. To the waitress, he said, "Put it on my tab."

She nodded and moved on to the next table.

"Thanks, Jack," I said.

He held his shot glass up in a silent toast, so we lifted our piña coladas. Then the three of us drank. Jamie almost poked his eye out with the red plastic sword holding his maraschino cherry and pineapple wedge together. I sucked from my straw. Jack emptied his shot glass and returned it to the tabletop. "Why are you two here?"

"Because it's the only bar for miles," Jamie slurred.

"It's spring break," I explained, "and we didn't want to go where everybody else went. Why are you here?"

He stared over my shoulder, perhaps looking at the sea again, before answering. "I'm waiting."

"For what?" I asked.

"For the tide to turn," he replied. He was silent for a moment, and then he said, "You ask a lot of questions."

I jerked a thumb at myself. "Journalism major."

"And your friend?"

Jamie had one arm on the table and was resting his forehead on it.

"Undeclared," I said.

"Five-year plan?"

"If he's lucky." Jamie was killing time until he inherited his grandfather's money, and college was just as good a way to do it as any other. I finished my drink and reached for Jamie's.

"Looks like your friend's ready to go back to your room," Jack said.

"I think we both are."

Jack had the waitress bring him an unopened bottle of whiskey. Then he helped me hoist Jamie to his feet and walk him to the exit, which wasn't anything more than a step down from a raised floor to a gravel parking lot.

"How'd you get here?"

"Walked."

"Your friend's in no condition to walk back," Jack said. "Let me give you a ride."

We carried Jamie to Jack's rental car, poured him into the backseat, and then I joined Jack in the front. I watched as he drove, and he watched the road. There were no streetlights to illuminate the two-lane highway, only the soft glow of a quarter moon filtering through the overhanging trees and the rental car's headlights slicing through the darkness ahead of us. Jack drove attentively, like a man who didn't think he would pass a sobriety test if he were pulled over.

When we reached our rental cottage, Jack helped me get Jamie to the bedroom and we dropped him across the king-sized bed.

"Are you staying here?" I asked. *Here* was six two-room cottages and a building containing the office and a kitchen that served a buffet breakfast and nothing else. We hadn't seen a maid the entire time we'd been there.

"No," Jack said. "I have a house farther down the beach." He told me which one. I'd seen it from the road on our ride from the airport. It wasn't a house; it was a villa.

"You have that entire place to yourself?"

Jack smiled wanly. "I do now."

I had no idea what the hell he meant, but I wasn't sober enough to pursue the conversation. Feeling dizzy, I steadied myself by grabbing his upper arm. Even wasted I appreciated the firm muscle I had wrapped my fingers around, and my cock stirred in my board shorts.

"You're a good-looking guy," I slurred.

Jack peeled my fingers from his arm and encouraged me to lie on the bed next to Jamie. When I did, I passed out.

I awoke the next morning to the sound of Jamie violently expelling the contents of his stomach. I pressed pillows to my ears but I couldn't completely block the sound. When I heard the shower, I climbed from bed and pulled on clean board shorts, a tank top, and my flip-flops. I left Jamie in the cottage and walked north along the beach until I came to steps carved into the face of a cliff that led up to the villa Jack was renting.

The villa's wide stone porch had a waist-high retaining wall on the cliff side and, after I climbed high enough to see over it, I found Jack sitting at a glass-topped table, nursing a cup of coffee. He'd seen me coming and had an empty cup waiting on the far side of the table. After I sat, he filled it from a silver pitcher and asked, "Why are you here?"

"Isn't it obvious?"

"You want to seduce me."

I didn't confirm or deny his supposition. Instead, I lifted the coffee cup to my lips and sipped.

"Do you always get what you want?" he asked.

"Usually," I replied. "Do you?"

"I do," he said, "but I can't always hold on to it."

He went inside and returned with a framed photograph of a slim blond with model good looks. "I thought Randal was the one," Jack said. "He didn't feel the same about me."

"What happened?"

"A relationship is like the tide. It ebbs and it flows. Right now the tide is out, but he'll be back." Jack paused and looked out at the sea. "I just don't know when."

I finished my coffee, thanked him and returned the way I had come.

Jamie had showered and dressed and was standing in front of the bathroom mirror fixing his hair. "Where've you been?"

"I went for coffee."

He glanced at my reflection in the mirror. "And you didn't bring any back?"

"I didn't eat," I said. "I thought you might want breakfast."

He did.

We spent that day exploring the island and we spent that night exploring each other. As we lay in bed afterward, Jamie asked, "You were thinking about him, weren't you?"

I turned and looked a question at him.

"You know who I mean," he said. "The swimmer."

I didn't deny it. "Why do you ask?"

"You didn't make love to me," he said. "You *fucked* me."

Jamie turned away and fell asleep with his back to me. I stared at the ceiling for the longest time, certain that this trip would not turn out the way Jamie had wanted it to.

Friday afternoon we crossed paths with Jack at a little restaurant in town. Jamie and I were sitting at a table outside, eating conch fritters and French fries, when Jack came walking down the street.

He saw us and stopped at our table. "Your week's almost up, isn't it, boys?"

"We leave tomorrow morning," I told him.

He turned his attention to me. "Not much time left," he said. "Did you get everything you wanted?"

"Not yet."

After Jack walked away, Jamie leaned across the table and grabbed my forearm. "What the *hell* was that all about?"

I made a dismissive gesture with my free hand. "It's nothing."

But it wasn't. That evening I took Jamie out drinking and made certain he downed two or three piña coladas to every one of mine. Then I hired a cab to return us to the cottage and paid the driver extra to help me manhandle Jamie into the bedroom.

After I was certain he was settled, I changed clothes and slipped out of the cottage.

Jack had watched me walking up the beach, and he met me on the back porch of his villa. He wore a blue silk robe and held two shots of whiskey. He handed one to me.

When he held his shot glass up, I touched the rim of my glass to his. Then we knocked them back.

I'd never had whiskey straight—I'd always had it mixed with diet Coke—and it made my throat burn and my eyes water.

"Man's drink," Jack said.

I didn't argue. Was I now a man?

We put our empty shot glasses on the retaining wall.

"You're leaving tomorrow."

I nodded.

"And you've come to make one last pass at me."

I wanted him. I had wanted him from the moment he walked out of the sea. I wet my lips and nodded.

There was no need to seduce him and no need for foreplay. We both knew what we wanted. Jack undid the sash and his robe fell open to reveal a thick, uncut phallus and the wild nest of black hair it sprouted from. I dropped to my knees, wrapped one hand around his rapidly rising cock and pulled back his foreskin to reveal the swollen purple head.

I took his cock in my mouth, hooked my teeth behind the glans and painted his cockhead with my tongue, soaking it with saliva. Then I slowly took his entire length into my mouth before I drew back. I did that twice more before Jack grabbed my head and face-fucked me. His heavy sac slapped against my chin each time he buried his cock in my mouth. When his sac began to tighten and his breath began to catch I knew he was about to come. I prepared myself for the geyser.

He came, firing thick wads of hot spunk against the back of my throat. I tried hard to swallow it all, but I couldn't. Some of it leaked out and dripped to the stone porch at my knees.

When his thick cock stopped spasming, he pulled away, took my hand, and pulled me to my feet. Then he shoved one hand into the waistband of my board shorts and pulled me close. He unfastened my shorts and they dropped to my feet. I wasn't wearing anything beneath them and my cock was already hard.

I peeled off my tank top, stepped out of my shorts and kicked off my flip-flops. Then he spun me around and bent me over the waist-high rock retaining wall so that I was facing the sea.

So that he was facing the sea.

He wet his middle finger and pressed the tip against the tight pucker of my ass. Before I could ask if he had lube, Jack buried his finger to the second knuckle.

I slowly opened to him, but he was impatient. A moment later I felt the spongy head of his cock press against my ass, surprised at how quickly he had gotten a second erection. He eased his cockhead past my sphincter and, once it was in me, grabbed my hips and thrust hard, burying his cock deep inside me.

My arm flailed out, knocking one of the shot glasses off the retaining wall. It shattered somewhere below.

Jack held me tight as he drew back and pushed forward. I braced myself against the wall with one hand and used the other to grab my own cock, pumping the engorged shaft in counter rhythm to Jack's powerful thrusts.

I came first, spewing cum across the rock wall.

Then Jack came again, firing a thick wad deep inside my ass. His body trembled as he held me pinned against the retaining wall, and neither of us moved until his cock softened enough to slip free.

Without a word, he took my hand and led me into the villa, up the stairs and into the master bedroom, a room big enough to play half-court basketball in, filled with heavy, oversized furniture. The French doors had been flung open for an unimpeded view of the Caribbean, and a light breeze tickled the curtains.

I excused myself to use the bathroom and, while washing my hands afterward, discovered a pair of toothbrushes in a cup and two different colognes on the counter next to the sink. Jack had not come to the island alone. I returned to the bedroom where Jack stood next to the open French doors, staring out.

"Where did Randal go, Jack?"

He turned. "Swimming."

"Alone?"

"No."

Before I could ask another question, Jack pulled me into his arms and covered my mouth with his. He forced his tongue between my teeth and kissed me so hard and so deep that it took my breath away.

Then he scooped me up, carried me to the bed and fucked me again, driving all other thoughts from my mind. After he finished, I fell asleep with Jack's powerful arms wrapped around me.

* * *

When the sun rose, I slipped out of Jack's bed and walked through the entire villa. I couldn't find him to say good-bye. I didn't have time to hang around, so I found my clothes on the porch where I'd left them, pulled them on and headed down to the beach. Nine steps into my descent I stepped on broken glass, and, at first, I thought it was my broken shot glass from the night before. Then I looked down and saw an empty picture frame—the same frame that had once held the photograph of Jack's handsome lover.

I hesitated. Jack was gone. The picture was gone. I was out of time. There was nothing I could do but go back to Jamie.

I walked south along the beach, back to the cottage.

As soon as I pushed open the door, Jamie shouted, "Where the *hell* have you been?"

"I went for a walk."

"All night?"

I didn't respond.

"You went to see him, didn't you?"

I didn't deny it. Instead, I finished packing. Then I had the front desk call us a cab. When it came, we shoved our bags into the trunk and sat in the backseat as far from one another as we could get. I sat seaside and stared out the window.

Halfway to the airport, a long stretch of the road hugged the shoreline, with only a thin stretch of white sand between the road and the water. Ahead of us, at the point where the road turned inland again, an ambulance and a trio of police cars with their lights flashing blocked the road. A dozen people had gathered on the beach, watching two paramedics working over someone or something.

A lone police officer stood in the road directing traffic. As the cab slowed, our driver rolled his window down and asked what all the commotion was about.

"A body washed ashore," the officer said. "Looks like a tourist got caught in the tides."

A tourist? Thin blond? Muscular brunet? I craned my neck to see but the cab moved forward and the crowd below shifted position to close the gap between people. I never learned the answer.

The flight home next to Jamie was long and uncomfortable, and we barely spoke a dozen words between us. As soon as the cab deposited us in front of our dormitory, we went our separate ways. A few days later Jamie dropped out of school.

I never saw him again. But I often revisit the image of a perfect man emerging from the sea.

HYACINTHUS IN BLOOM

Gerard Wozek

I am finishing up a box of hard candy hearts from last week's Valentine's Day. Each message passes quietly over my lips as I read them to myself then let the cliché sentiments dissolve on my tongue: BE MINE and KISS ME and COME CLOSER. All these clever taunts stamped on the side of each compressed confection melt onto my tongue as I stroll through the glass-enclosed botanical garden.

I found the little box of pink and beige saccharine hearts in the clearance bin next to the Safeway checkout. I could have offered a few to my coworkers or designed a clever ruse and left a handful next to my computer screen at the office and pretended someone had set them there just for me. But instead, I am taking them all for myself, sucking them down to pools of sugar syrup, as I brush past the newly budded larkspurs and garden house pansies, their bright petals tipping onto the drenched soil after a fresh watering.

I come here on my break from work to invent conversations I

imagine having with a newfound lover. I want to hear someone, perhaps another garden stroller I might encounter here, ask me to kiss, or offer a half-hushed enticement to linger skin to skin somewhere behind the exotic ferns. I want to taste the scent of roses on my imagined companion's neck, languish in a steamy wind spell of dahlias with him, then let the delicate perfume of baby mandarins and Italian blood oranges wash over us as we descend into a primal heat.

I am usually able to keep my full-blown fantasy of a man-to-man exchange of muscled embraces amid wet, languorous kisses and unbridled thrusts straddling somewhere between my subconscious and waking mind. But being here today, ensconced in the muggy Lincoln Park Conservatory, an oasis of tropical plants housed just to the north of Chicago's urban district, those covert, submerged impulses are offered freer rein.

There is something semi-arousing about the water slowly dripping down the cloudy glass panes of this aging greenhouse, the damp smell of the freshly fertilized soil and the artful way the moss is wilting down off the branches of the transplanted Florida palm trees and gingerly brushing the back of my goose-bumped neck as I saunter by.

The last heart that dissolved on my tongue had a hot licorice flavor. The taste of anise and cinnamon is sticky on the roof of my mouth, so I pop in a WILL YOU and savor a fresh burst of cherry infusion as I make my way toward the rear of the building. I pass through a narrow, rectangular area filled with tropical violets and hanging garden pots stuffed with dewy, overgrown succulents. It's nearly impossible to make out the classical composition piped into the greenhouse because of the intermittent radio static. The music buzzes through the ceiling then gets lost in the tangle of suspended foliage, as though the pulse of the plants is taking over the piped-in concerto.

At the end of the hall, I notice a dark-eyed groundskeeper with a raffish buzz cut, wearing a ripped athletic T-shirt and faded green-gray overalls. He is methodically rolling up a garden hose around the spigot of a clay aqueduct poking through a cracked stone wall. His sewn-on name tag reads GIACINTO, and as he turns to wind up the green piping, I dart a few quick side glances at his jutting derriere, then quickly look away, pretending to examine a steamy ground-level fern bed. He finishes coiling the snaky tubing around the spout then moves toward me with an alarmed jolt.

"Careful. You'll hit your head on that hanging grape ivy."

"Oh! I didn't notice it." I touch the side of the thick clay pot just above my forehead. "That could've been fatal."

"*Cissus rhombifolia* is generally pretty tame." My rescuer looks straight at me. "It's that heavy stone pot it's sitting in that might have given you a good bump on your head."

"So that's another name for grape ivy?"

"Grape or oak leaf ivy. Either one really. You can tell by the spindle shape of the leaflets." He gently holds a purple-colored tendril between his two thick fingers as he stands just inches from me. "This subtropical variety resembles the common grape leaf. Can you see the subtle variation?"

I touch the moist stem and my fingers momentarily graze his wrist. "Yes, I do see," I answer, nearly breathlessly, taking in his cleft chin, strong Roman nose, and dark, thick eyebrows and lashes. "It's just that, well, grape leaves make me think of my lunch yesterday near the Halsted Street Greek Town."

"This particular variety is imported from the West Indies." His soft breath is on my cheek, and he smells like cool summer field grass after a sudden drenching of rain. "So, are you a horticulturalist or do you prefer a pedestrian stroll through the plants?"

"Well, I am pretty enamored with all the connecting green-houses." My face flushes with blood and the humidity seems to have rapidly increased. "But I actually come here on my lunch break, for the subdued tempo and the sun."

"I love it, too." He nods, brushing away a bead of sweat from behind his left ear. "Especially in the winter, I love the ultraviolet light coming through the wide glass panels. It keeps everything in here warm and lush and growing."

"Growing, yes. I believe that it's even working on us," I say. My Italian-branded gardener winks and places a firm hand on my elbow.

"Have you seen the fifty-foot fiddle-leaf rubber tree in the center of the main greenhouse? It dates back to 1897."

"I believe I noted its thick trunk earlier." It's clear we're both sensing the same primitive vibe as we walk together down the brick footpaths wending toward our destination. My guide steps over the low wire fence and motions me to follow him onto the manicured flowerbed.

"Perhaps you've never seen the fiddle-leaf from this partic-ular vantage." He walks through patches of purple violets and clover then disappears behind long shafts of thick, dark-green foliage. I follow him into a natural enclosure crafted by long leafy branches crisscrossing over one another.

"You're right." I can barely speak and I'm not certain if it's my pulse thundering in my ears, or the heartthrob of the towering tree we're standing under. "It's magnificent up close."

"Just be careful," he whispers, pointing to a dribble of white sap oozing from one of the cut leaves. "This old rubber tree has just been pruned, and its juice can be pretty sticky. The stain is nearly impossible to get off of clothing."

"You seem to know quite a bit about plants. You must be the resident horticulturalist."

"My grandfather tended prickly pomegranate trees in Sicily. Every summer my father would take our family for an extended trip there, and we'd help him with the orchards. You just pick things up, that's all."

My tongue is still coated from the black cherry–flavored heart. Giacinto's dark eyelashes shade his hazel eyes, and his lips resemble the shape of the weeping fig tree's bounty, bursting next to us. The branches seem to dip lower around us as we huddle close to each other, my nose now nuzzling his damp chest hair.

"It's only us in here?" I try to keep my voice steady and quiet.

"It is only us." He slips his tongue into my mouth. "Ah. Hot sun-berry kisses?"

"I have another, but I don't know what flavor it is."

"I like your flavor just fine."

Dirt encrusts Giacinto's fingernails, but I don't mind. He smells like the earth, damp and grassy and fertile. His lips glide over mine and the hair on my neck stands on end. Our bodies become one with the ropey branches and umbrella-like leaves.

Centered within an almond-shaped cocoon of greenery, we become a fire of jungle instinct amid the vines and brush. Our tongues seek refuge in exposed musky armpits and on jutting nipples, then trace down the trail of soft brown hair coating our hard bellies. Behind the chalky, chestnut bark fiddle-tree, we move slowly, silently into each other. I try to keep my heavy breathing hushed as we collapse onto the craggy trunk of the sheltering tree.

The black-haired cherub cradles my head atop a bicep tattooed with a purple vine of tiny three-pronged leaves. I am damp from our shared perspiration and the oozing sap of the rubber tree that has leaked onto my forearm. A nimbus of blue-winged butterflies circles above us, then settles onto a long ficus branch to perch above our shiny shirtless bodies that have now reflexively folded into each other.

"Giacinto," my voice cracks, "I don't usually, I mean—this isn't typical. It's just, I have to see you again," I reach into the jeans knotted around my ankles and hand my blushing gardener my business card.

"Nice to meet you, Luke."

"As in Lukeois. I'm named after my father. I think it means wolfish, so you'll have to forgive me today for my lack of boundaries."

"I think we can make an arrangement to satisfy the wolf that roams within you."

"An arrangement?" I steady myself against the peeling bark of a dwarfed willow tree a few inches away.

"My partner, Zeffie, is caretaker of this place. I'm here every Monday and Friday to help him out."

"Your partner as in life partner?" The words float in the dank air, then evaporate like steam.

"I'm learning to untangle my life from Zeffie's sphere." He glances past a hedge of bushes that have been shaped to resemble a swan. "You can help me with this."

"Tell me how."

"We can meet together here on occasion. Create our own little legend, if you will, in this oversized greenhouse. If you'd like to."

"Here?" I study the spacious environs, then return to relishing Giacinto's handsome face. "You're saying, give up my lunch for a steady diet of your French kisses?"

A finger of sunlight passes through a clouded pane of glass and falls directly on our foreheads. It purifies us, galvanizes the palpable physical electricity that yokes us together.

"So, next Monday, then? Luke, please know I do wish we could be more open. But in time, perhaps?"

"Well, not every passion can see its way into the daylight."

"As long as I can stand in your light again."

"Half past noon under the rubber tree?" I note the sun has reddened his olive complexion, rendered his freckles more prominent, his brow more tan.

"I'll be waiting there for you, my cherry kisser."

I hand Giacinto my last hard sugar heart and turn down the footpath leading out of the conservatory.

"Why not?" The muffled laugh in Giacinto's voice disturbs the soft atmosphere of the plants as he calls out to me. I turn around and he's holding the tiny heart between two fingers. Then, smiling, he pops the Valentine into his mouth and turns away.

Thirteen clandestine meetings under my belt, so to speak, and I'm still handing my secret lover candy hearts—often just passing them to him from my tongue to his—but this time, I place it in his hand for him to read.

WHAT'S NEXT? Giacinto blushes and looks away.

"It's not that I don't enjoy our kisses behind the shade tree," I begin in earnest. "But I think it's become something more—for me, anyway."

"You can overwater the African violets." Giacinto points to wide terra-cotta pot of exquisite pink and purple blooms. "Too much pruning back, too much fertilizer, and they die. You have to give them just a bit of your careful attention, then allow nature to do the rest."

I run my finger down the nape of his wide neck to the crest of his broad right shoulder. "So you're saying, step back?"

"My tender wolfman, why can't this time here be enough?"

I flash on the last two months of covert meetings with Giacinto: My insistence on having a conversation each time in order to know him better. My gentle prodding to get details of his failing relationship with Zeffie. My repeated requests to meet outside of the conservatory, for dinner dates or walks along the lakefront. And always the same response: "Why would you want to leave our little Eden?"

What constitutes a real romance? I ask myself after each addictive session with my lover. *Does it only begin and end with an extravagant sexual embrace—or does there have to be a mutually shared zeal to know one another—a desire to share one's secrets and become accustomed to one's habits, both the charming and annoying?* Maybe Giacinto is right—maybe it's enough just to linger beneath the dripping glass ceiling of the conservatory all afternoon and create our own insular mythology of passion and desire.

People come to the conservatory to absorb the beauty of the exotic plants, to breathe in the aroma of the dwarf roses, to marvel at the color and shape of the Peruvian lilies, to brush against the tendrils of the hanging fern plants. But there are signs everywhere forbidding the visitors to pluck the blooms. "Perhaps it is enough," I say out loud to myself, walking to another interlude with Giacinto. "I don't need to bring home a bouquet of iris—it's enough to gaze at his beauty, to appreciate his perfection."

I enter the warm sanctuary of trees and flora. Walking up the stone path, I note that Giacinto is arguing with a stocky, dark-skinned, middle-aged man with a shaved head and wide penetrating eyes. His nostrils are flared and sweat beads Giacinto's knitted brow.

"You're just a lot of wind. You think I care about your threats?" Giacinto is shaking a mud-clotted garden trowel in his adversary's face. "You're just filled with a lot of hot air, Zeffie, so why don't you just blow out of here already."

I step lightly past the agitated couple, between two rows of yellow tea roses. Giacinto swiftly moves past me beyond the sightlines of his oppressor, nods silently and with a jerk of his shoulder motions for me to follow him.

We move through dripping moss and low-hanging branches into an area off the public path that is notably and unusually humid.

"This way, my hungry little wolfhound." Giacinto has already unbuttoned his overalls and pulled his sleeveless T-shirt over his head. "We have to hide our scent." We push through the narrow opening of a large bush into a remote corner of the greenhouse. Rows of potted plants sit upon a wire wall shelf: hibiscus, bright red azaleas and a bird of paradise, mute in cracked crockery.

"Unbuckle yourself and let me see how faded your summer tan lines are." Giacinto pulls at my belt buckle and playfully kisses my forehead.

"Who were you fighting with?" My voice wraps around the dense tree branches above my head, heavy with crescent-shaped leaves.

"Don't concern yourself with that. He's nothing." My Italian beauty reaches over his head and begins to do chin-ups onto the branch above. "Count for me, Wolfie."

By the time I get to sixteen, Giacinto's workpants have fallen from his body and rest at the base of the sturdy tree. He wraps his legs around my neck and shoulders, and I sequester my face in the warm crevice between his hairy, muscled thighs. The ocean-salt smell of his moist crotch blends with the clammy air of the covert garden.

"Listen, I'm a little nervous here. Let's talk."

"We're safe," he assures me with a hushed puff of air from his lips, then pulls himself onto the wooden chin-up branch. "Have you ever done it in a Bald Cypress tree, my friend?"

"You mean, like the monkeys do?" I whisper as Giacinto extends a hand to me and hoists me onto the splintery perch. The tree's branches are intertwined, forming a giant canopy above us, shutting out the sunlight.

"It's a sky of branches up here," I say, reaching up for a neighboring limb.

"The *Olea europaea* is this tree's next-door neighbor."

"Translation please?"

"Just an ordinary olive tree, my little wolf," Giacinto says, plucking an overripe green seed from the tip of the branch, "also known as a moira. They're common on the Isle of Crete. Been around for thousands of years, as old as myth."

"Do you follow the legends of the great gods?"

"I'd like to think their stories are still in us, Luke. Like a genetic code, their thumbprint is planted inside of us so that, perhaps, we're destined to learn their lessons."

"The gods broke all the rules, though, Giacinto." I slowly kiss the tips of each one of his exposed toes. "There were repercussions for that, even on Mount Olympus."

"Always consequences, my gentle coyote." Giacinto shrugs as he climbs higher into the maze of branches. "For every action, a reaction. Everyone knows that truism."

As we move together through the tangle of leaves and curving branches, a beam of sun somehow burns through the thick foliage.

"How is it that even in the center of a tree there is sunlight?"

Giacinto places his hands on my warm face. "It is wherever you are, Luke. With you and all around you, pure, perfect light."

He deftly steps onto the next branch and dangles his manhood just above my face.

"So this is part of your tree-climbing sport?" I rest my back against a smaller upper trunk and steady myself on a short branch. The inner sap from the tree hums and throbs and merges with my own. I marvel at Giacinto's athletic frame, his perfectly sculpted torso, his sinewy, muscled arms entwined with the thick network of branches.

"If we climb any higher we'll be meeting Zeus," I call out.

I stand at a lower branch and it's enough to kiss his ankle, taste the salt perfume that emanates from his body.

"Careful, I might fall for you," he grins back at me.

"Giacinto, I already have, for you."

"Should we build a little tree house here, my friendly hound?"

I try to secure myself onto the next highest branch. All of the trees around us shudder with my shifting weight. "Maybe it could be our own little rendezvous point—something more permanent for us," I concur, then I reach for the spindly trunk of the tree in order to gain better equilibrium.

"Steady yourself here in my arms, Wolfie." Giacinto reaches from behind me, one arm around my waist, the other hand extending in front of me. "Can you see that top shelf of flowers on the wall there?"

I note a row of tiny budded flowers in soft purples and creams lining the ledge. "They're exquisite," I say. "I love the small cone-shaped petals."

"It's my namesake flower, you know. Those perennials are of the genus Hyacinthus. They originated in Anatolia and were brought to Europe in the sixteenth century."

"You were named after the flower?"

"I was named after my grandfather. But he and I are both connected to that plant—he taught me how to cultivate them. He had a greenhouse dedicated to every type: the brodiea, the squill and the deathcamas. I used to wander for hours up and down the aisles, watering the soil, gaping at the purple and white petals. He inspired me to make a life out of working with plants."

I crouch and step down a level to get closer to the fragrant blooms. "I can almost smell them from here," I whisper.

"You should be able to get a good whiff of them now because I just heard the vent fan turn on overhead." Giacinto rests his head on a long branch under his neck.

I move carefully down the massive tree, then step back onto the ground and move closer to the petals.

"You know, hyacinths are cultivated in Holland for the perfume trade." Giacinto speaks in a normal voice, enough to be heard above the rustling branches and grinding air vent.

"Could we go to Holland together?" I call out as I quickly step back into my crumpled wardrobe. "I'd love to watch you pick out tulip bulbs there."

"We could go anywhere together," he answers slyly, "as long as I can pick out your big bulb anytime I want.

"Ah, you say that. Don't make promises."

"It's not a promise, just an image to focus on for a moment," he replies. "Can you toss up my pants? Careful of the garden tools strapped onto the heavy belt strap. Just ball them up and I'll catch them."

I toss the crusty heap of denim and metal tools up toward Giacinto's perfectly toned and naked body. I turn back to the hyacinths, and take down one of the terra-cotta pots holding the blooming bulbs. I sit cross-legged under the tree while Giacinto fumbles with his trousers, pulling out a small cutting tool.

"One second, I want to see if I can reach this one stray branch."

There is a great deal of jostling about in the bramble of leaves above me. I hear the snapping of twigs and the tumble of heavy branches falling onto the hard ground. I listen as Giacinto gasps, as though all the air had been taken out of him.

Without warning, a pair of ratchet pruning shears falls to the ground, then Giacinto stumbles off the branch he is standing on and falls in a heap at the base of the tree.

I am dumbstruck. Terrified, I see bald-headed Zeffie, pale and quivering, climbing to the base of the neighboring tree trunk. He collapses at the gnarled roots.

"I'm telling you, it was an accident." Zeffie is shaking wildly and placing his sweaty hands over the wet gash on his partner's forehead. "I was pruning back the branches of the old elm tree. I didn't see him. I swear I didn't see what I was doing with those cutters."

I watch as the hulking figure begins to quake over the still body of my Giacinto. His breath comes out in wild spasms and meshes with the whooshing wind of the fan overhead. Dazed, I note that small flecks of my secret lover's blood have speckled the soft-hued petals of the grounded hyacinth.

"My sweet wolfhound..." Giacinto is barely breathing. "Seems we've both been tracked down—ambushed, if you will."

With the fight-or-flight instinct kicking in, I move back through a tangle of low flowering bushes. Stumbling over the rutted earth, I graze a spigot pipe sticking up in the ground, as my whole body lunges onto the footpath.

I can't shake the heady scent of the hyacinth plant. From the corner of the greenhouse, I hear Zeffie's unsteady voice stuttering into a cell phone. "I need an ambulance. Right now, someone hurry, please."

My instinct is to flee, to find a place to howl and thrash about. But I'm completely winded and instead lean against a vine-covered trellis at the threshold of the conservatory's front entrance. The sun overhead has scorched the potted plants lining the circumference of the bright patio, turning the thin tips of their petals a tobacco brown. I note how frail and delicate the veins of the leaves are; their exposed green, so delicate and vulnerable. I close my eyes but all I can see is the vague pink of Giacinto's blood mixing with the palette of the hyacinth's orange-purple petals.

I try to imagine the details of the conversation we had just moments ago: intimate, bare, sentences layering over one another like the soft pat of a shovel in a planting bed. Our words and gestures and intentions, like a scatter of seeds waiting for water and sun and the frail spark of germination.

What were the words he used? Hold me? Speak my name? Don't let go?

My thoughts are jumbled. *This was just a clandestine affair—it wasn't a real romance—it only existed within the boundaries of this greenhouse.*

I try to make sense of the cacophony in my brain. How did Giacinto's voice sound? How was it made distinct with all the blooms and beehives humming all around us? His phrasing was so gentle, sometimes barely audible, that we always needed to stand close; his voice always meshing with the wet air, the classical music station, the intermittent sunlight.

Perhaps I was in the grip of the Stendahl syndrome—that odd psychosomatic illness that produces confusion and dizzy hallucinations when individuals are exposed to too much beauty. Giacinto's voice, his presence, his embraces had become for me a kind of sickness, a disease that produces intoxicating music in the brain. That was the only way to describe my infatuation with him, the way one would try and describe the sound of violin strings and mournful cellos—as if one could ever.

I was sick, of course I was, lovesick—lost in the exquisite, unworldly notes of Giacinto's voice that braided around all these exotic plants and trees and this persistent tropical steam.

I steady myself against the trellis and note a stark white bloom placed at the exit to the greenhouse. I begin to recall vague details from a college course in Greek mythology that remind me that Hyacinthus was a divine hero who was deeply loved by Apollo. In the classic tale, Hyacinthus is struck by a wayward discus and dies. Apollo is so bereft that he creates a flower, the hyacinth, from the youth's spilled blood.

I am not Apollo and I don't have the power to disallow hell from claiming Giacinto—or rebirth him into a magical flowering plant. But I do have this strong desire, this urgent need, to rescue him—even if there is a jealous lover looming amid the spiders and geckos in the foliage.

I inhale deeply and turn around to face the path back into the conservatory, the trail that wends toward the thick mesh of leaves where Giacinto's body was splayed. "So beauty has its own rules," I tell myself. "It gives the seduced individual the ability to act on behalf of the seducer."

I walk faster and begin to imagine bringing Giacinto back to a restored state of calm. I imagine visiting him in the hospital, bringing him potted orchids that he will explain are vulnerable to drafts. He will caress their petals and teach me exactly how much water to give them, how to tell if the soil is moist enough, how to place them just so at the windowsill.

"It is fated," I say aloud to the wilting snapdragons.

I touch my forehead and wipe off the ring of sweat. The sun seems hotter, the graying glass enclosure more humid. I reach into my pocket for a handkerchief or a tissue, something to blot the unrelenting perspiration, but there is nothing except a half-melted hard candy heart from last week.

"I could have sworn I had swallowed every last one," I say to myself, and I take it out and press the still hard surface between my fingers.

TELL ME, it mocks. But at the moment I am unable to form words. I cannot speak the incantation that will bring Giacinto back or call on the disdainful gods for mercy and redemption. Apollo was able to spare Hyacinthus from entering Hades. Is the strength of a budding romantic adventure enough to save Giacinto?

I inhale the heady scent of lilac and convince myself that when I turn the corner, just around the thicket of Japanese chestnut trees, Giacinto will be waiting for me, conscious and breathing, with enough spark and pulse and fire to heal.

I assure myself that when our eyes meet, somehow I will find the consoling words that will bring him back to me, so that alive and together we will reinvent the old parable, rewrite the outworn ending of the tragic Greek myth.

I take another step, put the last candy heart in my mouth and bite down hard.

BEAUTY, MATE

Barry Lowe

What was it that people saw in me that made them think Andrew and I would hit it off? He was gorgeous and the boy most likely to be pursued in a bar. He was intelligent, belonged to various gay political organizations and thought the older generation, of which I was a perfect example, had crippled the gay movement with our hedonism and our lack of political will.

He had flawless skin if you ignored the cluster of pimples around his chin—and it was easy to ignore those slight blemishes on an otherwise perfect complexion. His eyes were what you noticed most. Or was it his smile? His hair, the way it hung over his forehead and spiked at the crown?

And here he was screaming abuse at me in public along Oxford Street, Sydney's gay Golden Mile.

"You're so fucking tragic," he screamed as a few guys passed by smirking, probably mentally calculating the difference in our ages (*It's only twelve years*, I felt like screaming. *He's twenty and I'm thirty-two*) and marking me down as a premature sugar daddy. "You don't have an original thought in your fucking head. Everything you say is vomited up from opinion pieces in what passes for quality journalism in this city. It's all shit! You're shit!" And to emphasise his point he threw his arms out to encompass the street on which we were currently the top entertainment, "And all this is just commercial bullshit milking the gay proletariat's dollar."

A few people stopped to applaud and, if I hadn't been on the receiving end, I might have applauded as well. But he had the wrong man. He hadn't taken the time to find out who I was. I had marched in gay rights demos in which the police had beaten up protestors. I'd been outside homophobic companies and church dioceses when men had been fired for their sexual predilection. But, of course, Andrew didn't know that. We'd only met half an hour earlier.

We'd taken an instant dislike to each other.

"Go home, granddad," Andrew said, his energy finally draining out of him. "Your time is gone. Let us take over now."

"It's all yours and you're welcome to it," I bellowed back as I slunk away, leaving half a dozen predators hovering in hopes of picking over the remains of our short-lived friendship. Ah, the fickle nature of gay life—and the fickle transience of beauty.

I wasn't ugly. I just wasn't young and beautiful anymore.

Back home, I slammed the front door in frustration.

"You're home early," Nathan said and got up to give me a hug as comforting as only a long-term boyfriend can bestow.

"Opinionated little prick!" I spat it out and felt better for it.

"Didn't go well then?"

"Thinks he knows everything! Has an opinion, no matter how half-assed it is, on anything I brought up. Oh, sure, there's an inquiring mind in back of that pretty little head of his...."

"You didn't say anything *about* his pretty little head, did you?"

"I might have."

"And you didn't make the mistake of telling him how young he is?"

"Um...well..."

"And just exactly how did you take it when people said the same things to you back when you were his age?" Nathan asked.

Nathan always did have a way of putting things in perspective.

It was two or three weeks later when Andrew and I met again. It wasn't planned. Our house was always open for friendly drop-ins because we were so close to the center of the gay metropolis; to people passing on their way to parties, to the bars, on their way home. Nathan and I had just finished dinner with two close friends when another, Tony, and his entourage turned up at the door. And who should be among that entourage but Andrew. I smelled a rat and suspected Tony was attempting to precipitate another conflagration between the two of us, having heard the gory details from the bush telegraph that swept Oxford Street.

There was a buzz to the ad hoc gathering, about ten people in all, not least because of the buzz of exploitative interest in Andrew. He was instantly the focus of the crowd's attention; everyone in the room was subtly and not so subtly attempting to impress him. There would be heartbreak tonight.

One of Andrew's friends had staked a claim and was hovering possessively at his side, while others circled flirtatiously. I was never a fan of blood sports, so I left the room to replenish wines and make coffees and teas. Soon enough, I was chuckling as

I heard voices raised and laughs shrieking more volubly than usual and people's words tumbling over one another, all in an effort to dazzle Andrew. From my vantage point a room away it sounded shallow and futile.

"Can you do anything?"

The question took me by surprise, and I only realized when I looked up that the voices in the living room had subsided. That was because Andrew was in the kitchen speaking to me—quite civilly, as it turned out.

"What's the problem?" I said.

"They all want to fuck me," he said.

"My, aren't we the modest one." I couldn't stop myself from a little payback.

"I should have known," he said as he turned to walk away.

"I'm sorry," I said, and I was. "I know they are. I could hear it from here."

"Any solutions?"

"You'll hurt a few people's feelings," I said.

"That's okay, I seem to manage that anyway," he smiled and that smile said it all.

I dragged him back into the living room and the noise level rose once again.

"Okay, everyone. Listen up," I said in my most authoritarian tone. "Andrew's a bit uncomfortable with all the attention, and while he's flattered, the situation is awkward. So, how about I ask Andrew if he's interested in each of you one at a time and those who get the nod can slug it out and the rest can just chill out. Okay?"

There was ready agreement. The fear of public humiliation was overridden by the hope of anointment.

Very carefully I went around the room, giving Andrew time to weigh his response about each eager man—which was always a warm but final No, even to my other half, Nathan, and, emphatically, to his overtly infatuated hanger-on.

When it was all over he'd turned down everyone,

"Now you can all relax and enjoy yourselves," I told them.

I started back toward the kitchen to finish assembling the drinks, but Andrew interrupted. "You haven't asked me about *everyone*," he said, smiling.

"Who didn't I ask you about?" I said.

"You."

Everyone in the room looked at me expectantly. I was the only person who had shown no interest in Andrew. I didn't like whatever game he was playing.

"Okay, Andrew. For the record, are you interested in me?"

I'd already turned and was halfway down the hall when I heard him say, "Yes."

Not what I'd expected.

People suddenly realized how late it was or how tired they were or else were just so pissed off they couldn't stand it, and the house emptied quicker than an inflatable sex doll with a pin prick. Nathan gave me a peck on the cheek and whispered, "Lucky bugger," as he went off to bed. The only person who resolutely refused to leave was Andrew's leechlike hopeful, who sat peevishly, casting a pall over our enthusiasm and interrupting our very personal snogging with sarcastic observations about my shortcomings for about twenty minutes. We carried on as if he weren't there, and—at last!—he huffed his way out the door.

I swept the hair off Andrew's pale forehead and leaned down to kiss his pimples.

"No one's ever done that before," he said, wistfully.

I unbuttoned his shirt slowly as I moved from his chin to his mouth, running my tongue across his pink lips, which parted to receive me. I gently probed his mouth and sucked in his tongue with just enough force to mean business. I found his nipples and ran my thumb across the pink-brown nubs. He shuddered his appreciation, and I bent down to lick and bite them lightly.

His cock sprang to attention and I ran my fingers along the outline in his jeans before I unbuttoned and pulled them, along with his briefs, down over his tight butt. He peeled off his shirt so that now he was naked. His body was perfection: a swimmer's body, slim but muscular, not overblown.

He settled semiprone on the settee, luxuriating—I assumed—in my stare. *He knows he's beautiful and my gaze is his due*, I thought. I ran my fingers over his chest and belly deliberately teasing his cock, which jolted as I neared it. I turned him over and traced the outline of his spine. His body delivered the tactile sensation of a beautiful marble sculpture.

I slid my finger between his asscheeks and sought out his hole. It was moist and I knew it would taste sweet. I parted his legs and pushed my face into the crack, easing in my tongue. He groaned and began to stroke his cock, but I swatted his hand away.

His cock was musky as I ran my tongue around his knob to lick away the light layer of precum. I tongued down the ridge under his cock to his balls, sucked them into my mouth and washed them with my saliva. I was worshipping him like priceless porcelain, careful lest he break, and he was responding like a beautiful object—as a perfect body, but not as a turned-on person. My sexual ministrations were one sided. He lay passive. I was doing all the work. I wanted sexual reciprocation.

I stood and stripped off my clothes as seductively as I could; Andrew watched, at first without reaction, but he must have eventually liked what he saw because he beckoned me to come back to him. He took my cock in his warm mouth and leisurely sucked me into his velvet throat. I turned my body to keep pace with him, and we eagerly devoured each other's prick. I couldn't hold off much longer, which he must have sensed: "I like it on my face," he said.

I stood up and over him. He looked so vulnerable.

"Shoot it on me. Blow your load on my pretty fuckin' face," he groaned, pounding his meat with a sudden, surprising ferocity.

I jerked my cock and it didn't take long because his tongue had already brought me close to the edge. I shot strings of warm spunk across his face, in his hair, and even a few squirts in his mouth, which opened in ecstasy as his own cock spewed over his stomach.

"Rub it on me," he begged.

I ran my fingers through the puddle of cum in his navel and smeared it across his face and lips. He sucked my fingers clean and I soothed my own cum into his forehead and hair, then leaned in to kiss him, tasting our comingled juices.

"Now, piss in my face," he said as I fetched a towel.

"Why do you want that?"

"I hate being good looking," he said, and I detected a bitterness in his voice that I'd previously missed—or ignored. "Most guys won't do it. They don't like the idea of defiling beauty. Pissing on me is almost the equivalent to them of defacing a work of fucking art. I'm not a work of art. I'm more than a beautiful body. I'm a person."

I picked him up and took him to the bathroom and laid him in the tub, then released a bursting bladder of beer onto his face and into his mouth, finally soaking his hair.

He smiled, contented. In that moment, through the shower of hot piss, he was more beautiful than most people would ever see.

A LITANY
OF DESIRE

Dan Cullinane

Like floods. Like fires. Like droughts and ice storms and oceans and rivers and desert landscapes. Washing, wasting, wilting, waiting. Like cities at night and open roads under Wyoming skies and bridges reaching into the sky. Promising, postponing, pointing.

There was Joe, all those years ago, sitting on the floor in Randy's trailer, his eyes on the TV watching Peter Gabriel sing "Sledgehammer" on MTV. I watched the spirals of hair disappearing up his thighs into the shadow of his shorts, and I wanted to follow it to places I had never been but knew I wanted to understand.

There was Jim, who lay under a tree in Duncan Park, shirtless and laughing, tipping his head back to empty his beer, and spilling it. Desert mouthed, I watched the spill run down his chin and into the hollow of his neck, and farther into the curls of hair on his chest. I was scared of what I wanted, and I didn't move, and I averted my eyes. There were people surrounding us, and I wanted bad things to happen to all of them. I wanted to lap the beer on his chest, and I didn't want to know that that was what I wanted. Late one night, I fell asleep in Jim's house, and when I woke my head was in his lap, and he was smiling down at me through miles of darkened living room. Planets were born and civilizations fell in the moments between waking and when his head found its way to me, and I wrapped my fingers in his blond hair and tasted his bourbon and his cigarettes.

Desire is a mirror and I am nothing or no one without its reflection. Desire shines and lies and flickers like Saint Elmo's fire. It leads you forward and it leaves you in the dark and you can still feel it glowing.

There was Steven, who pushed me backward over the bar at the Gallery in Baltimore and kissed my neck before returning to the pinball machine. It was our first date, and afterward we took an endless taxi ride through night streets to his basement apartment, and I wondered if I would ever enjoy fucking, because it seemed like nothing but pain. But falling asleep made it worth every inch he forced into me. He kissed me like a starving man, over and over, on street corners, in restaurant booths and at the end of the pier overlooking the harbor. He towered over me and he moved like mercury, and being naked with him was as close to love as I had ever known, and when he vanished I burned for him and learned what a squirrelly bitch desire is.

There was Michael, who jerked me off in the front seat of his car in an empty parking lot in Dundalk, while his lover was at home dying of AIDS. I followed him from place to place, taking whatever small things he had to give, showing up at the garage where he worked and eating lunch with him in the alley. He took me to the beach, and I gave away whatever pride I still had over dinner with his friends, who stared at me and wondered how I could be so inhuman. I was sick for his crooked smile

and the way his hair flopped over his forehead and for the way
he told me we were two peas in a pod. It didn't matter that
nothing would ever move forward and that the front seat of his
car would always be as good as it could ever be.

There was Dan, who kissed me under the spinning lights on
the dance floor at the Hippo, and I kissed him back because my
ex-boyfriend loved him. I don't remember his face, not anymore,
but I remember his lips and his taste, because they felt and tasted
like winning. He took me home, driving fast and dangerous up
I-95 and braking, smoking and screaming, at the end of the off-
ramp. He looked at me funny when I got out of his car, and I
smiled and said good night, and I walked up the walk without
looking back, and the tires squealing when he pulled away from
the curb gave me chills.

Untrustworthy and unworthy. Along the way I learned to set
it aside and sought out something less. When the fire was cold,
it was safe to move forward, so I lived with men who I never
wanted to touch. Sex was penance for lying and payment for
safety, and when I got caught I did it again and again. Until
it stopped working, and I found myself again chasing the blue
flame across the horizon.

The savage, singular beauty of men is their relentlessness.
There is nothing I have that can't be taken, and it is in the taking
that I find my rapture. It is always a surprise to find out how
much more there is.

There was a guy who pulled my hair back and kissed me by
the pool table at the Brit in Long Beach. He grabbed my wrist
and dragged me to the door as people around us laughed and
cheered. I felt tossed and owned and I was drunk so I didn't
question it. I rolled with him, naked in my bed as he fed me his

iron cock, and forced my mouth down onto him until I choked. I had watched him playing pool, and I had caught his eye. What he saw in me that made him want to bitch me out like that I didn't care. The stale beer odor rising from the floor and the bathrooms that always smelled like puke made me feel filthy, and I wanted him: his mustache and his powerful body and his white trash raspy voice, and the way he spit his beer into my open mouth in front of everyone, like I had no choice. I smiled. He lifted my legs and pushed inside me and grabbed my head and forced it onto his nipple, and I ran my tongue over the metal spike that pierced him and he whispered, "Nurse, baby..." and I did, and it was everything.

There was Michael, who took me to watch a sunset over the Pacific and told me that tonight was the night we would have sex. He told me his pizza theory about sex, how if you eat it when it first arrives you can burn yourself, but if you wait too long it's chewy and cold. He was imperfect and shorter than I was, but I looked at him, at his bright eyes and black hair and the way he never really smiled, and I didn't care whether the time was right or wrong. Later, as he leaned over me, buried inside of me, and kissed the inside of my legs, he whispered, "What am I going to do with you?" I wanted the answer to be forever, not because it was right but because it was there, and it ripped me apart and hollowed me out over the months, and when it was over I lost my bearings and drifted in the dark.

There was a man who negotiated me away in a sex club in Alphabet City. He was fat, and he was old, and when he kissed me I could feel the hair on the mole on his lip. But he stripped my underwear off and spanked me in front of a circle of guys who stroked themselves as my flesh grew pink and mottled. One by one he told them what they could do to me, and they did, and I lost myself on a wave of use that shocked me and left me panting and dizzy and starved for oxygen, and he pulled me out from under and held me until I stopped shaking. And I dropped to my knees and I gave him my service because he saved me.

Saved me.

It's opportunity and it's education by an elusive teacher. Fire burns but it also illuminates. Floods destroy but they also purify. Roads to nowhere are also roads to somewhere.

There was a guy whose face was pitted and hollow from the effects of protease inhibitors, but whose long bony body settled over me like a comforter, and who stroked me for hours as the sun went down through the patio windows. I never knew his name; he never bothered to mention it. His skin was brown and his scalp was tattooed and his cock was enormous. He licked my back and settled himself there and fucked my spine, and I stretched like a cat and inhaled his sweat. If we'd been in two separate rooms it would not have mattered, we were so given over to the satisfaction of our own sensations that we became invisible to each other. It was wordless and selfish and we both came hard.

There was Scott, who was straight and leaned out of the window of his red pickup on a street in Manhattan and kissed me. Ginger haired and runner taut, he offered himself to me as his first, and I took him facedown on my bed, pushing myself to give him something to make it worthwhile, and he shot over my pillows and collapsed smiling and sweating in my arms and fell asleep while I lay awake and stared at the ceiling and wondered if I had ever enjoyed sex like that. We met up in Provincetown one summer and walked through the artists' shacks out in the dunes and took off our clothes in the sun and gave ourselves over to the joy of limitless possibilities because we knew we had to make something out of what was never going to be possible.

Along the silent paths of years I return to the fires, and to the men who light them. We are older, and our passion is more complex and less easily tossed aside. We have worked and earned the right to ask for what we want.

There was quiet David, who made love to me next to a towering shelf of books, his hands moving over me like clouds, while my eyes drifted to the titles beside me until he noticed and took my jaw in his hand and returned my attention to his laughing face. David, who was lean and light and whose armpits I could never get enough of licking; David, who took his pleasure in silence, rarely talking, waiting to cry out as he shot into my mouth while sucking on my toes.

There was Tom, who shattered my complacency by kissing me all around the room, and who ran his hands over my body as I drank in the sight of his. Tom who made me feel new, and who made me wake up, and who made me think about where I was and what I wanted. Tom, who fired a full magazine of affection in my direction, and who reminded me of Silverlake in 2001, except this was Asheville in 2009. He was all razzed-up energy and oversized sunglasses and Diesel jeans and mannerisms of urban hipsterdom that had guttered out long ago. I wanted to say, "Baby, I did that in L.A. years ago, I'm not that now," but I didn't, and all I thought about was the way it felt when he touched me, and the way it felt to fall asleep with my cheek pressed into the tight and scratchy curls of hair on his beautiful chest.

There is a way to connect. There is a way to be grown up. And there is a way to find my way to the center, to the fire, to the touch, to the kiss, to the giving over. There is a way to do all that and not give up. But I wanted to. I wanted to forget it all and to give myself completely to a man who was still finding his center. I could see the rain coming, and I watched it and recognized it, and when he vanished, and the rain arrived I did not burn out.

Desert landscapes and open roads, ice storms and floods.

Elusive and flickering but not unworthy. There it is, again, on the horizon. Words on paper and a voice on the phone and no idea of the man's body. Strong words, words that have touched me long before I knew there was desire for me. Words that embraced me as I struggled back to my feet. A voice that laughs in my ear and tells me stories. God, how I want this man. And he is coming toward me. And all that I have learned, and all that I have cast off, makes me open. At last.

ABOUT THE AUTHORS

MICHAEL BRACKEN's short fiction has been published in *Best Gay Romance 2010*, *Biker Boys*, *Country Boys*, *Freshmen*, *Homo Thugs*, *Hot Blood: Strange Bedfellows*, *The Mammoth Book of Best New Erotica 4*, *Muscle Men*, *Teammates*, *Ultimate Gay Erotica 2006* and many other anthologies and periodicals.

ERIC DEL CARLO (ericdelcarlo.com) has been published in numerous anthologies over the years, most recently in Circlet Press's *Queerpunk*. His novels and novellas are available at Loose Id. Look for new work in *Best Erotic Fantasy & Science Fiction* and *Only in the City*.

DALE CHASE (dalechasestrokes.com) has been writing male erotica for more than a decade, with one hundred twenty-five stories published in various magazines and anthologies, including translation into German and Italian. Her first story collection, *If the Spirit Moves You: Ghostly Gay Erotica*, is from Lethe Press.

DAN CULLINANE is a freelance writer and teacher in Eastern Tennessee. He has been published in various Cleis and Alyson anthologies and is blessed to combine two aspects of his life: the written word and outdoor adventure, teaching etymology, literature and creative writing to students in the beautiful Blue Ridge Mountains.

JAMIE FREEMAN (jamiefreeman.net) has known many truly beautiful men in his life. This story is for his good friend, the beautiful Jonathan. Jamie's stories have appeared in a wide variety of anthologies and e-books.

BARRY LOWE's (barrylowe.net) short stories have appeared in *Cruising for Bad Boys*, *Surfer Boys*, *Hard Hats*, *Time Well Bent*, *The Mammoth Book of New Gay Erotica*, *Flesh and the Word*, *Best Date Ever*, *Boy Meets Boy* and others. He is also author of *Atomic Blonde: The Films of Mamie Van Doren*.

MATTHEW LOWE (matthewlowe.com.au) is a young Australian writer. His work has appeared in a number of journals and anthologies, including *Best Gay Romance 2008*. A recipient of an Express Media Mentorship Award, Matthew's work appears here alongside that of former mentor Andy Quan.

PHILLIP MACKENZIE, JR. is an occasional writer of raunch for fun and profit. His stories have appeared in *Hard Drive* and *Boys in Heat* and in the late, lamented *Freshmen* magazine. He divides his time between Los Angeles and Tennessee, with long stretches behind the wheel of his pickup.

TOM MENDICINO spent six raucous years eking out a living in the sales departments of several New York publishing houses before attending the University of North Carolina law school. Since 1994, he has practiced as a health-care lawyer; his debut novel, *Probation*, was published in 2010.

ANDY QUAN (andyquan.com), Canadian-Australian, is the author of one collection of short fiction, *Calendar Boy*; two of poetry, *Slant* and *Bowling Pin Fire*; and one of gay erotica, *Six Positions*. His work has appeared in a broad range of anthologies, magazines and literary reviews in Australia, Canada and elsewhere.

SIMON SHEPPARD (simonsheppard.com) is the author of six books, including *Sodomy!*, *In Deep* and *Hotter Than Hell* and edited the Lammy-winning *Homosex*. His work appears in more than three hundred anthologies, and his weekly column "Notes of a Cranky Old Fag" is online at CarnalNation.com. He absolutely loves beautiful boys.

CECILIA TAN is the author and editor of many books of erotica, including *Boys of the Bite, Edge Plays, Royal Treatment* and *Magic University*. Two gay novels are being published serially on the web, *The Prince's Boy* weekly on circlet.com, and *Daron's Guitar Chronicles*, three times a week on daron.ceciliatan.com.

ROB WOLFSHAM (wolfshammy.com) has appeared in several anthologies, including *Best Gay Erotica 2010, Muscle Men: Rock Hard Gay Erotica* and *College Boys: Gay Erotic Stories*. He lives in Dallas, Texas.

GERARD WOZEK is the author of the short-story collection *Postcards from Heartthrob Town*. His debut collection of poetry, *Dervish*, won the Gival Press Poetry Book Award. He teaches creative writing at Robert Morris University in Chicago.

ABOUT
THE EDITOR

RICHARD LABONTÉ (tattyhill@gmail.com) was a gay book-seller for twenty years, has written book reviews for more than thirty years and has edited about thirty gay anthologies (mostly erotic) for Cleis Press and Arsenal Pulp Press. He lives on Bowen Island, a short ferry ride from Vancouver, with husband Asa Dean Liles—who, despite meeting Richard in a gay bookstore, is not a reader, though he's happy to bring packages with book galleys and finished books home from the post office. Several editions of the *Best Gay Erotica* series, which Richard has edited since 1996, have been Lambda Literary Award finalists, and two have won, as has *First Person Queer* (Arsenal Pulp), coedited with Lawrence Schimel.

More Gay Erotic Stories
from Richard Labonté

Buy 4 books,
Get 1 *FREE**

Muscle Men
Rock Hard Gay Erotica
Edited by Richard Labonté

Muscle Men is a celebration of the body beautiful, where men who look like Greek gods are worshipped for their outsized attributes. Editor Richard Labonté takes us into the erotic world of body builders and the men who desire them.
ISBN 978-1-57344-392-0 $14.95

Bears
Gay Erotic Stories
Edited by Richard Labonté

These uninhibited symbols of blue-collar butchness put all their larger-than-life attributes—hairy flesh, big bodies, and that other party-size accoutrement—to work in these close encounters of the furry kind.
ISBN 978-1-57344-321-0 $14.95

Country Boys
Wild Gay Erotica
Edited by Richard Labonté

Whether yielding to the rugged charms of that hunky ranger or skipping the farmer's daughter in favor of his accommodating son, the men of *Country Boys* unabashedly explore sizzling sex far from the city lights.
ISBN 978-1-57344-268-8 $14.95

Daddies
Gay Erotic Stories
Edited by Richard Labonté

Silver foxes. Men of a certain age. Guys with baritone voices who speak with the confidence that only maturity imparts. The characters in *Daddies* take you deep into the world of father figures and their admirers.
ISBN 978-1-57344-346-3 $14.95

Boy Crazy
Coming Out Erotica
Edited by Richard Labonté

From the never-been-kissed to the most popular twink in town, *Boy Crazy* is studded with explicit stories of red-hot hunks having steamy sex.
ISBN 978-1-57344-351-7 $14.95

Ordering is easy! Call us toll free or fax us to place your MC/VISA order.
You can also mail the order form below with payment to:
Cleis Press, 2246 Sixth St., Berkeley, CA 94710.

ORDER FORM

QTY	TITLE	PRICE
_____	_____	_____
_____	_____	_____
_____	_____	_____
_____	_____	_____
_____	_____	_____
_____	_____	_____
_____	_____	_____

SUBTOTAL	_____
SHIPPING	_____
SALES TAX	_____
TOTAL	_____

Add $3.95 postage/handling for the first book ordered and $1.00 for each additional book. Outside North America, please contact us for shipping rates. California residents add 9.75% sales tax. Payment in U.S. dollars only.

* Free book of equal or lesser value. Shipping and applicable sales tax extra.

Cleis Press • Phone: (800) 780-2279 • Fax: 510-845-8001
orders@cleispress.com • www.cleispress.com
You'll find more great books on our website

Follow us on Twitter @cleispress • Friend/fan us on Facebook